For *Jacob*, *Kieron* and *Daniel Twine*,
with love – my original unholy trinity!

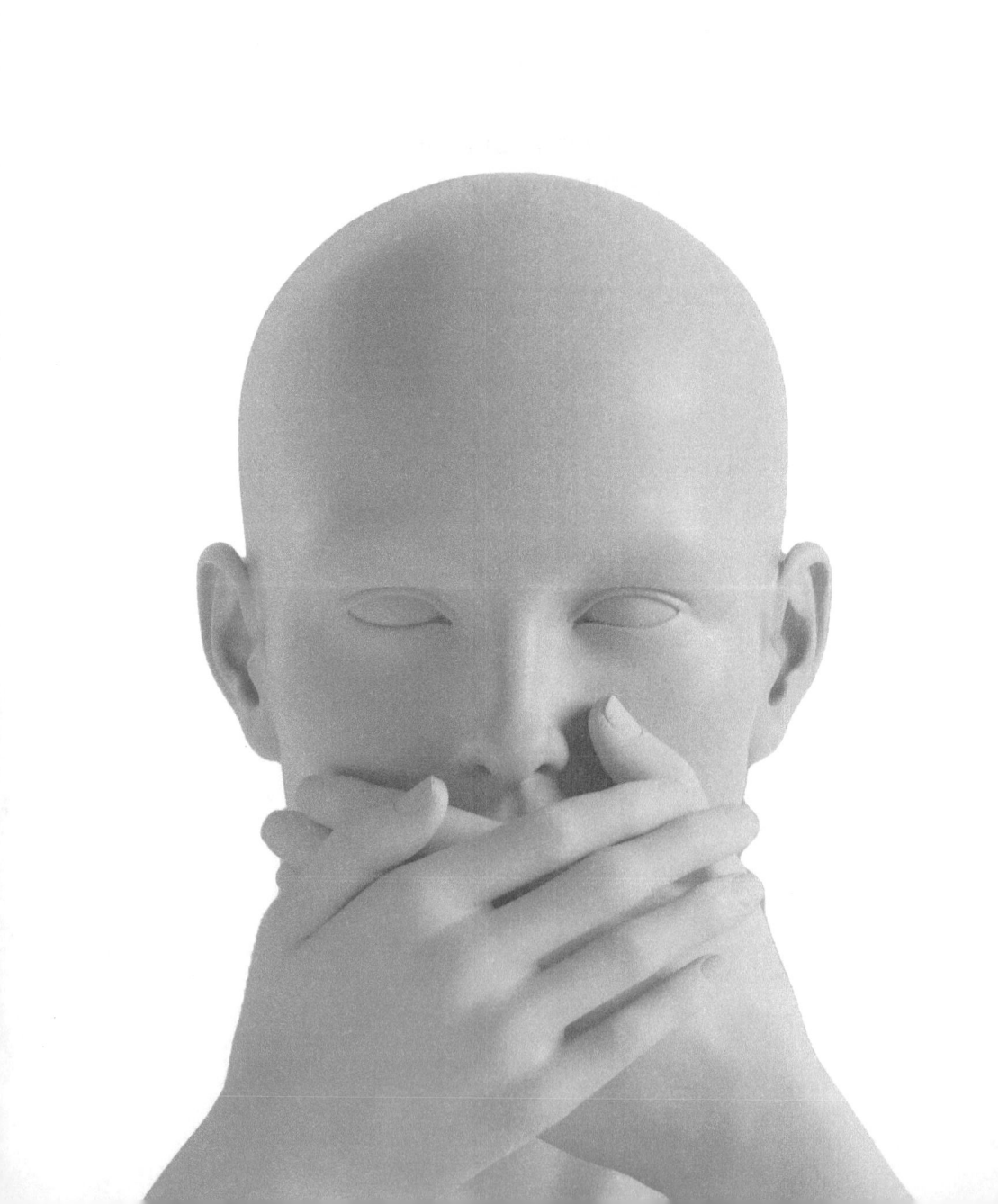

ANNIE FLANAGAN

DUMMY RUN

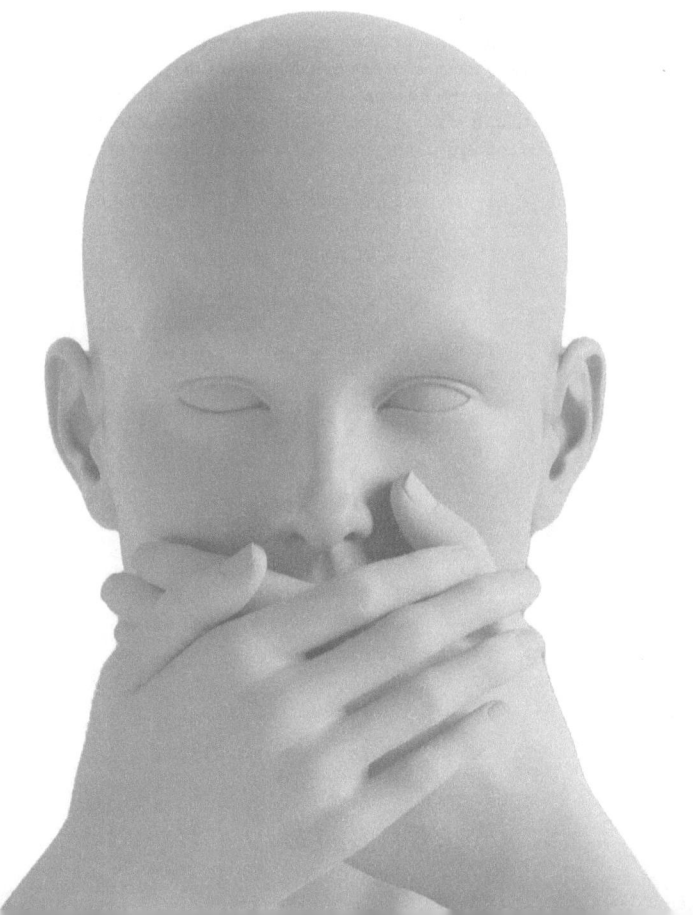

Editing, design, typesetting and publishing by UK Book Publishing

www.ukbookpublishing.com

ISBN: 978-1-915338-16-7

Chapter 1

I don't know about your school, but mine is absolutely brilliant at some things and total pants at others. Lunches are great but the dumplings are a bit like depth-chargers, the Performing Arts Department is cool, especially when we're allowed to get into the recording studio, but that's only to watch the girls in the Dance Studio next door: and the bell for home always goes bang on 3.15. All round, not bad. But let's not get too worked up.

Assemblies are a snore-fest, none of the experiments in Science set fire to anything interesting (like the nerdy NQT) and Work Experience is a complete disaster, for some. In theory, it's a great idea: us teenagers off school for two whole weeks, doing exciting things, sometimes even learning new stuff and, once in a while, getting paid for it. In practice, however – D'oh!

This is how *my* school placed us bright eyed and bushy tailed lot in their placements. Kirsty, who was a shining star in all the aforementioned school productions, fancied going into the theatre as a make-up artist. Her work experience placement was at an Undertakers. I mean, really? My mate Gaz wanted to 'work with animals' cos that's about his limit, but bless him, he ended up in a butcher's shop. Jeremy Vincent, who scores straight As in everything he does, had aspirations to become a Marine Biologist: poor Jeremy ended up working at the fish quay, unloading shoals of herring. Honestly, you couldn't make it up. They did get it right with Little Stu though. He ended up in a local Racing Stable, was taken on as a stable hand in the holidays and weekends and may yet surprise us all by becoming a champion jockey.

We did laugh at poor old Jacob Johnstone though. He is a quiet lad who has always looked about 25 instead of 15. The beard helps of course. He was working in the hospital as a porter. On one shift he was mistaken for a second-year medical student and was just in the process of removing some stitches from a head wound when the real doctor arrived. He enjoyed the haberdashery department at Dooley's after that shock though.

Some of the clever kids, who really put their heart and soul into organizing their own placements, had a brilliant time. One of them went into local radio and even went on air doing the traffic and travel. Can you imagine the fun and the damage you could do with *that* slot, eh?

My mate Rob went into a sports shop, and while he got great discounts on all the Premier League football kits, he actually came out hating the Great British Public and vowed the closest he'd ever want to be near to them again was on the pitch, playing for a top-class team. So, he'll have to move away from Sunderland then… I really tried to find something interesting, challenging and entertaining, but as usual left it too late.

Eventually my sister Jilly stepped in to help. She was the one who got me the work experience placement at that stupid shop. She thought it would be really funny to see me spend two weeks as a window dresser, taking the clothes off dummies, where all my mates could walk past in their lunch hour and could stand and have a right giggle while they ate their chips. SOOO embarrassing. I was the talk of the town. Everyone started calling me Wanda the Window Dresser and would put on a really effeminate voice when I was around. That just made me determined to make it work for me. I had a cunning plan. Some way or another I was going to get my own back on Jilly for putting me in this situation. I mean, all I had done was tell her boyfriend that she used to wet herself at the first few bars of the "Jaws" theme tune. Did that really merit me getting all that grief?

Some of the lads had job placements in garages, or print shops, or in the local nick, or McDonald's, and there was me, bright red, taking tights off frozen faced mannequins and reapplying their lippy. Honestly! Jilly was going to get it right up her jacksy for that! All right, I could have chased up the job at the railway yard, but I couldn't face working with Mad Mick, the security guard. Him and me had a history, a love-hate relationship. He loved to hate me and the lads, and vice versa. We'd been the bane of each other's lives for years. I couldn't give all that up and go to work with the guy. It would be like crossing over to the Dark Side. The gang would never forgive me. I mean, who would we drive crazy on a Saturday night if I made friends with Mad Mick?

Anyway, because it was a toss-up between the railway yard and Dooley's Department Store, Jilly got in first and applied for me, as a joke, for showing her up in front of her boyfriend. She had it all planned, the witch!

For the first day I was stuck in the offices at Dooley's, doing Health and Safety, little bitty jobs like answering the phones and making tea. The staff were all right. Lots of bright young girls buzzing in and out, smelling of perfume and winking at me. I thought, wahey, this is going to be alright. Having an older sister has some good points after all. Wait till I tell the lads.

I fantasized about the little, dark cute one with the curls inviting me for a drink after work and me saying, well, ok, just the one. I have to take my fiancée to the theatre tonight, but I won't tell if you won't. I mean, what's one Sex on the Beach between friends? She wouldn't know that I was only 15 of course. I'd tell her to meet me outside of the Cross Keys as I had to drop the Porsche off at the garage for its service. Oh, this was going to be fun.

It was the morning of the second day that our Jilly really put the boot in for me. She breezes into the office with the snotty under manager's assistant in tow and says,

"This is Will, my brother, the one I was telling you about."

I saw that sly wink, you madam. "He's always had an artistic bent." A what? "So I thought he'd be just *perfect* in windows." Next thing I know I'm there for the whole world to see, changing the bra of a dummy in the Winter Wonderland display with some sweaty 60-year-old store assistant with halitosis. You are SO going to die for this, our Jilly!

Of course, in a perfect world, bras and 15 year old boys are a match made in Heaven, but when half of the year 10 football team stops at the lights outside of the store's big front display window and sees me, Will Green, battling with one, it all takes on a different slant. All right, they were plaster boobs, and not real ones, but they WERE boobs. Probably the closest I'd ever get to the real thing anyway. Especially now, with my reputation in tatters. I'd never live this down. The bra in question was bright pink, like my face, and I think I'd put it on upside down. The busy-body who was helping me gave me a withering look. Well, how was I supposed to know? I was standing there, with half the town witnessing my shame and embarrassment, when I heard the roars of laughter. Even through the thick pane of glass I heard them shrieking in delight. I glanced up and there they were: the school football team on their way to a match in the mini-bus. Well, what could I do?

The red light seemed to be stuck! It certainly held the bus there for ages with all the lads leaping about for a better view, posing, taking photos and blowing kisses at me through the window. Ok, I thought, in for a penny in for a pound, as they say. As the lights changed and the mini-bus began to move off, I suddenly grabbed the model by the boobs with both hands and planted a big smacker on her cold, clamped lips. I could hear the disbelieving roar all the way down the street. The mini-bus nearly tipped over as the boys all raced to the back window to cheer and wave at me in delight. I smiled and gave a victory salute.

Well, that's what I told the angry-looking granny window assistant I was doing.

"Everybody's got to start somewhere, haven't they?" I asked her, grinning.

The rest of the fortnight wasn't too bad, and I began to enjoy myself. It wasn't exactly rocket science and the staff were all great fun. Plus, I had free ice cream and coffee from another mate who was working on that counter. I wasn't always in the window. Well, not after I positioned one of the male models in a compromising position with the female model wearing the new nightie, I wasn't. They were like that for three days before some customer saw it and complained. I got away with it because I said Rolf must have fallen on top of Sheena like that.

Oh yes, I gave all the dummies names. The window supervisor thought I was weird, but it made sense to me, better than referring to them as the blonde one, or the cross-eyed one, or the bald one. I spent some time mending their injuries when they really did fall over in the storeroom and would pretend I was Charlie off Casualty, giving them injections and shouting stuff like "35mils of adrenaline" and "sub cutaneous haemorrhage". What a laugh.

One day Eddy, who was one of the main technicians in the store, like a caretaker really, asked me to take three "dead" dummies out to the skip. He said that they were old-fashioned and that a new batch was coming in. I wheeled them out in a trolley and chucked the first one into the skip. He hung over the side, watching me sadly with his cold blue eyes, his nakedness gleaming in the dim light of the back yard.

"Don't look at me like that, Nigel," I told him. "I'm just doing as I'm told. I know you'd be happier in a nice warm bed, but it's not up to me, is it?"

That's when I decided to "borrow" Nigel, Flora and Keith. I stashed them away behind the bins and began raking about for anything to wrap them in.

Ten minutes later I was back with some bubble wrap and had found two old wigs and a brown Flasher Mac for Keith. But, hang on a bit; there were now four of them. I swear I had only left three dummies behind the bin. I stood there, scratching my head and gazing warily around in case one of the other kids was playing a trick on me. Jilly, maybe? Nope, I'd just seen her, simpering around the new young area manager. And Jeremy in Haberdashery didn't have the intellect or the humour to add a fourth dummy. Odd, and a bit spooky, if I'm honest.

Dooley's back yard had very high walls, topped off with razor wire, so it was always gloomy and grey, even in the summer. There was a selection of industrial sized bins, some old storage sheds, boxes lying everywhere, and old wardrobes leaning drunkenly against the walls. The seagulls didn't even venture into this yard, but I know for certain that rats and mice loved it. I shuddered and moved towards the partially hidden dummies.

I was counting the legs, but there were eight, when I know I had only left six sticking out, some wrapped in old newspaper. What the...?

I crept forward, my knees slightly bent, fists clenched at my side. I was ready for anything. At the first sign of a rabid rat or vicious seagull I was outta there. I mean, if I'd had my posse with me, it would be different, the lads would have my back; but I wasn't expecting a lot of help from the three naked dummies lying on the ground behind the bin.

"Ok, you lot. I know what you're up to. Get up and get out of here before I call security," I called out in as big a voice as I could muster. I tried to sound like Tyson Fury but it probably came out more like Mickey Mouse.

Suddenly, one of the feet moved, and at the same time something shifted inside the bin and toppled over with a metallic crash. I leapt back, crashing into an old filing cabinet, which also wobbled about, rocking backwards and forwards like a demented Dalek. Grabbing it, I called out, "Right, you lot! That's enough now. I'm coming in!"

Ee, Will man, give your head a shake, I told myself, silently reminding myself there were four of them behind that bin. I stood there, breathing heavily through my open mouth, visions in my head of a battle royal with three wild-eyed, naked dummies and a fourth, as yet unknown, assailant. Maybe their evil master? What if he had armed them all when I went to find their wigs? I paused in my tracks for a second: this would actually make a really good computer game, maybe I could make a fortune on this – I'd better get my mobile out and leave myself a reminder...

Someone giggled. I turned my head slowly towards the sound. My shoulders dropped, and some of the tension drained away from me. Ok. Now, dummies can't laugh, any more than they can get up and ambush a 15-year-old in all their naked glory. As I looked on incredulously, the one moving foot became two, then a pair of grubby hands joined it, and someone started giggling and singing at the same time.

"I'm forever blowing bubbles, pretty bubbles in the air."

The voice was elderly, wobbly and totally oblivious of trying to hang on to the original tune. The huge bin moved and swung around on its castors as the person behind grabbed hold of it and hauled himself to his feet, tripping over the naked dummies on his way. He chuckled again, belched loudly and staggered from his hiding place, long grey hair blowing in the breeze, torn trousers at half mast, a grubby hanky waving about like a white flag, in surrender.

"Jimmy! What on earth are you doing in here?" I asked him, reaching forward to hold the old man up, but not actually wanting to touch the dirty old guy. I felt myself easing down from some of the terror, well, *surprise,* I'd been feeling. I'm not that much of a wuss – honest.

Jimmy Jesus, as he was locally known, was a bit of a legend in his own backyard round these parts. All of us kids knew him. He was homeless, living rough as best he could. Many people took pity on Jimmy, feeding him, giving him clothes and pointing him in the direction of the local homeless charities, but nobody could keep him for long. Jimmy invariably escaped, despite everyone's best intentions, and seemed happier doing his rounds and sleeping outside. He was funny and harmless, always singing and bumbling about. Nobody had a clue how old he was, or how long he'd lived like this. He was just our Jimmy Jesus, and we all did our best to look out for him.

The man himself staggered out from behind the bins, clutching a bag full of mouldy doughnuts in one hand and a half empty bottle of some amber liquid in the other. I didn't look too closely at that, just in case. Jimmy stood on one of the legs of a dummy, almost fell, and then apologized profusely to it, leaning forward and patting it ineffectually on the head. He turned his watery grey eyes to me, made a "shushing" noise and put his finger to his lips. Pointing down to the three naked dummies on the ground he slurred at me, quietly, "Best leave 'em there. Shush. Let 'em sleep. They've had a lively night by the look of 'em."

Well, you'd know more about that than me, mate.

Sighing with relief that it was only Jimmy, and not some of Mad Mick's cohort out to bash my brains in, I guided him towards the open back door to Dooley's yard, holding my arms outstretched at my sides, talking to him gently as he stumbled ahead of me, still singing and wobbling about. *I should have had a pig-board in my hands,* I thought to myself. Certainly smelled like I was in a farmyard... Poor Jimmy.

When Jilly arrived to pick me up at home time, I told her to meet me round the back as I was taking some old stock for use in the school Drama department. She was in a hurry to get home to see Stupid Steve, the boyfriend, so she didn't take much notice as I bundled them into her boot. I'd had to remove their legs and arms first and I winced and apologized to them, but at last they were heading for home. I grinned to myself all the way, thinking of the fun me and the lads were going to have with this lot.

***

"Mint!"

Robbo's eyes nearly popped out of his head when he saw the dummies sitting on my bed.

"What are you supposed to do with them?" asked Gaz. "Bit squashed in there for the four of you, isn't it?"

He's not the brightest bulb in the box is old Gaz.

"Oh, they're not staying here, lads. We are gonna have some fun with this little lot," I told them. "Get your thinking caps on."

Robbo's always up for a laugh. He could see their potential straight away.

"You've got to take them to school tomorrow," he laughed. "He can wear my old uniform." I thought Keith's cold eyes seemed to flicker with interest. "Does your sister still have her old uniform for whats-her-name there?" he asked.

I looked at Flora.

"Well, she's taller than Jilly, but all the girls are wearing really short skirts again this year, so maybe we can fix her up."

Gaz was beginning to click on now.

"Yeah," he muttered. Oh good, we were getting through to him.

"Really short skirts," he mumbled. I punched him hard on the arm. It usually does the trick.

"Wake up Gaz," I told him. "We've got to put a plan together."

***

The next morning Robbo, Gaz and me arrived at the school gates carrying Keith between us. The dummy was wearing his uniform like everyone else and he seemed to blend in with the crowd, which I thought really odd because he looked like someone had dug him up from somewhere. I thought it said a lot about what us teenagers look like first thing in the morning. Anyway, none of the staff on late duty at the main gate thought anything was wrong – which says a lot about the state most teachers are in first thing in the morning too. Soon one or two of the kids started giggling and giving us three the eye, but they were wise enough to not cause a scene. Keith just stared straight ahead and ignored everyone. Well, he would, wouldn't he? We decided to put him to the first test.

We were just approaching the boys' toilets when a voice from behind called, "Where do you four think you're going?"

It was Miss Hawkins. Hawkeye, on duty. Obviously, her glasses were steamed up again.

Without stopping I called back over my shoulder, "Toilets, Miss. Curry last night."

"Too much information, Will Green. I'm timing you."

We hurried on, trying not to jiggle Keith too much with our laughter.

Inside we sat him on the toilet and pulled the cubicle door shut. Gaz was sent to find a prefect. He returned in a minute with one of the upper sixth, tugging at the boy's sleeve.

"Ah come on, mate. Hurry him out of there. He's been in for ages and I'm dying for a sh…"

"Shouldn't you call for a teacher?" asked the prefect. "This kid might be ill."

"He did look awfully pale when he went in," I told him, looking serious. Well, I wasn't lying, was I?

"OK lads, stand back. I'm going to kick the door in!" shouted Robbo, dramatically, lifting his foot.

"No, you're not. I'll see to this," replied the prefect, pompously. He climbed up the outside of the toilet door and peered over the top before sliding back down to us.

"You're right. I think he's really ill. He's slumped forward as though he's passed out," he told us, wide eyed with concern.

"Maybe he's dead," I said, slowly, milking it for all it was worth. The silence hung in the air between us as we all stared from one to the other, waiting for someone to make a move.

"That does it," announced the prefect. "I'm going for the headmaster."

It cost us two pounds fifty, a packet of cheese and onion, and a promise to put in a good word with our Jilly to get him to drop it. Eeh, prefects. They have far too many principles these days.

We were happy with the way Keith had been received on that first morning, but we decided not to push our luck. So as not to arouse suspicion that day we took him to the Hall and sat him in front of the baby grand. We decided that even if anyone came in, he would just look like the new music teacher practising for assembly.

I spent a few minutes reassuring Keith that I wouldn't go home without him. He looked a bit lost at first, so I placed a hymn book in front of him. Gaz shot me a quizzical look.

"There, he won't be bored now," I explained. The lads seemed to understand. I knew they would.

The four of us enjoyed the ride home on the bus. In fact, the journey wasn't nearly as rowdy as it normally is because the kids were fascinated by Keith, but I sensed one or two of the year sevens thought he was probably a spy for the senior management team. Hmm, he could have a future there, I mused. Stick him in uniform and sit him next to an old lady and she could travel in peace anywhere. We could earn a fortune.

That night me and the lads held our weekly meeting of the SGA in the boardroom – well, my bedroom actually. That's because I'm chairman and founder member of the SGA, which stands for Sad Gits Association. (For some reason Gaz always sniggers when I use the word "members" to address the lads officially.)

We decided that as Keith had been such a success that day, we would swear him in as a member of the gang too. It seemed churlish to leave him out when he had fitted into the team so readily. One look at that pale face of his and we knew we couldn't just leave him sitting forlornly on the pouffe in the corner whilst we three made plans for our next great escapade.

"Anyway, he's listening," Gaz announced, watching Keith warily.

"So?" I asked. "Let him listen. He's not going to tell everyone what we're up to, is he?" I asked, shaking my head at Gaz.

Robbo seemed to be gazing closely from each one of us as we spoke, like he was at Wimbledon. Then he dropped his voice to a whisper and turned his back on Keith in his corner.

"Hey, what if he's a spy? You know, like for Big Bird, or even your Jilly?"

Gaz quickly looked up in Keith's direction, his eyes wide in his head, then he ducked back down to whisper as well.

"I never thought of that! What shall we do now?"

I took a deep sigh, looked seriously at the two of them and beckoned them to bend in closer so they would hear my quiet voice.

"Tell you what. We'll jump him, you know, beat a confession out of him. Gaz, you pin him down, Robbo, you stop him from screaming for help, and I'll kick the stuffing out of him."

To my complete amazement they both nodded solemnly. Oh Lordy, if that's what it was going to take.

"OK then, after three. One. Two... Three!"

Well, as you can imagine, all hell broke loose at that point. In the melee that followed, my bedside lamp got kicked over, the wardrobe door flew open and all the clothes that I had flung in most carefully tumbled out on top of us, and someone stuck a finger in my eye. We were rolling about, all four of us, screaming bloodcurdling battle cries and punching and pulling at anything we could get our hands on. Then we realized what we were up to and stopped abruptly.

"Ha, lads, look!" Robbo pointed to the scene staring at us from the floor length mirror on the inside on the wardrobe door. Through my one remaining eye I could see total chaos. Gaz had a rip down the front of his tee shirt, mine was wrapped up around my neck and I had claw marks down the front of my belly. Robbo's jumper was twisted round and he had great red welts around his neck where *someone* had strangled him. And Keith's trousers were gone. His wig was hanging over one eye and one foot was in the waste-paper basket. We grinned in delight at the scene then started giggling. The next thing we were collapsed in fits of helpless, eye-watering laughter, rolling around on top of each other and gasping for breath so much that we didn't hear the door open.

"What the …?" It was Jilly, standing there in amazement. She surveyed the scene in front of her incredulously, looking from each one of us in turn. Robbo turned bright red under her gaze: he had always had a thing for our Jilly, daft sod.

"You … Perverts!" she exclaimed. "Wait till Mam hears what you lot have been up to in here."

We began to protest, but it was in vain. Her Highness had decided that we were all doomed for our unspeakable acts and looked at us as though we were something she had trodden in.

"We were just messing about, Jilly. Don't be such a stuck-up cow."

"This will cost you dear, baby brother," she announced. "That must be, oh, at least 15 quid you owe me by now."

Huh? How come my every misdemeanour ends up with me paying my sister for silence? Robbo jumped up to try to save my hide.

"Tell you what, Jilly. As it's you, and because there's a sale on this week, you can have both of us." He looked like he was doing her a big favour.

"What are you on about?" she asked him, suspiciously.

"Don't charge Will for this, take it out on me and Gaz. You can have us both." And he winked lasciviously and nudged Gaz in the side. "Two for the price of one. Bogoff. What do you say?" Then he winked again.

"Weird. Just plain weird," Jilly replied slowly as she backed out of my room, watching us three really carefully.

After that we tidied up a bit, dressed Keith again, played on my PlayStation and ate jam tarts while we plotted the next day's entertainment. Later, seeing the lads out of the front door, the three of us stopped and gazed down the garden towards the shed.

"Does your Ross know about the dummies yet?" Rob asked, quietly.

I noticed Gaz dropped his head and his face turned a funny shade of pink. He shuffled his feet about, hands stuffed in his pockets.

"Not yet," I replied. "I'll go down there soon though, once I've tidied up upstairs. I'll tell him then."

Gaz lifted his head and gazed at me levelly. "He'll be well impressed, mate," he said.

I smiled back at Gaz. "He will indeed," I told him. "See you tomorrow, lads."

Chapter 2

Next day it was Flora's turn. We had decided that seeing us lads around the school with a *girl* may prove to be unusual, so we tried to make her not as beautiful as we would have liked. That wasn't too difficult. Although she had a stunning face her wig looked like some item of roadkill that had been scraped up, and her left eyelash kept falling off. I swear one leg was slightly shorter than the other, but I mean, come on, there's laws about that sort of thing these days. We wouldn't hold that against her. And the way Robbo kept staring at her made me think he quite fancied our Flora.

I had hunted out Jilly's old uniform and we all agreed Flora suited the school colours much better than Jilly ever did.

"What size do you reckon she is then?" asked Robbo, looking closely at her.

"She's got a size ten printed on her bum," I told him. The lads looked shocked for some reason.

Gaz took in a huge intake of breath.

"Have you been in her knickers then?" he asked, incredulously.

I smiled at him. "Seen it all, mate," I told him with a wink.

"I meant, what *bra* size do you think she is?" Robbo explained patiently. Gaz began to stare at Flora's chest. I held a blazer protectively in front of her.

"Oh, like I'm going to raid our Jilly's undies drawer for a bra!" I stated. "I like having both ears you know. Flora doesn't need a bra. She won't be taking her clothes off in school now, will she?"

I thought they both looked a little crestfallen at that, but they knew it made sense.

The school bus driver, Eddie (yes, another one) thought Flora was a bit of all right but the rotten sod still charged us an adult fare for her.

"You're not telling me she's only 14," he said, sarcastically.

As we carried her up to the top deck there were one or two wolf whistles from downstairs and I caught a grotty, spotty youth trying to look up her skirt.

"Oy, watch it!" I demanded.

Gaz leaned in close to the kid. "Pervert," he snarled menacingly.

The kid coughed nervously. "Sorry, Gaz, I was just trying to …"

"Come back when you're a big boy and I'll introduce you to her sister."

We managed to get the front seat upstairs and the four of us got settled. I sat with Flora and put my arm around her to keep her steady. It felt weird: she even smelled like a real girl, probably because she was wearing Jilly's clothes. Unlike a real girl, however, she didn't rabbit on about EastEnders and who should have been chucked out of Love Island. Out of the window I could see other lads in my year doing a double take down on the street whenever they happened to glance up in our direction. I couldn't resist kissing her cool left cheek.

Robbo tutted loudly. "Cut it out, you two," laughed Robbo, "you'll make everyone jealous."

Next thing was this harsh voice whispered in my ear and a bony finger poked me in the back.

"Wotcha, Will. Who's yer friend then? Don't think I've met this slapper yet."

Marvellous. Just who I had NO wish to meet on the day I had Flora with me. Bernice Broadman, otherwise known as Big Bird or

Broadwalk, the bully of year eleven. I sighed and groaned inwardly. Gaz and Robbo were off their seats like a shot, standing in between Flora and me and the gorgon herself. Bernice, I mean.

Robbo blocked her view.

"Well, if it isn't the beautiful Bernice!" he exclaimed giving her his widest smile and bowing to kiss her hand. Blurgh!! Give that man a medal! I didn't dare turn round but I also couldn't help giggling. Gaz started flashing a smile too, but he just looked like a gargoyle. It put Big Bird off me for a minute though.

"'Ere, what's the matter with your mate? His face has gone all funny," she said, drawing herself up to her full five feet ten. I could smell the stale smoke on her breath, and I was still some way away – thank God.

"He's just dazzled by your beauty, Bernice," Robbo told her. "Don't you know, half of our year thinks you're the best thing since Kylie? Now if I was you, I'd give the poor lad a few minutes to recover. He's got a Maths exam this morning and you appearing before him like this could ruin his chances."

"Oh, shut your face, you," she declared. "I only wanted a word with the new girl there. Haven't seen her around before."

"She's very shy and nervous, Bernice, but how kind of you. Tell you what. You come to the Technology block at break, and we'll make sure you get to know everything about her. Ok?"

Bernice sort of slumped. We were coming to the corner shop where she had her breakfast of vinegar crisps and a Mars Bar every day. She knew she had to get off and leave us. Or starve. Her stomach made the decision for her. As she lumbered down the stairs, followed by her coven, she called back.

"You'd better not forget. If you're not all there it'll cost you, big time. And her. I'll find her. A new girl isn't easy to hide, you know." She clumped loudly down but on the bottom step she paused, holding up the gang on the stairs for good effect.

"She'd better not be laughing at me either!"

This was followed by some half-hearted snarls from her henchmen then they were gone, onto the street, where they pushed aside an old lady and a group of about five little 'uns waiting to enter the sweet shop. I raised one of Flora's hands and gave Bernice a cheery wave as the bus pulled away. I just stopped Gaz from pulling a moonie at her as well.

"Oh no you don't," I said, grabbing his waistband. "We're in enough trouble now already."

Gaz didn't seem bothered, but then he's not really bright enough to understand the implications of what had happened.

"Now, lads, don't get yourselves into a state. Our Flora is going to be just fine. You'll see. Make sure you get her to the empty cookery room in Technology as soon as the bell goes for break. Then leave it to me." He smiled, knowingly, and winked at Flora who simply gazed back as if she didn't have a care in the world. I wasn't going to be the one to burst her bubble then.

***

Flora seemed to enjoy Science, which is odd; I didn't have her down as being brainy. Our Science teacher, Elvis (Mr Presley to you and me), is a good sort who can take a joke. He allowed her to sit in his seat whilst he demonstrated something spectacular with a fishy-smelling gas and a Bunsen burner. Soon it was break and Robbo and me managed to beat the other kids out of the door by telling Elvis we had to deliver Flora to the Drama department.

When we got there, luckily Gaz was waiting and there was no sign of Big Bird and her gang. Gaz seemed keyed up.

"Right you three," he began, "see that oven over there? Get Flora and lie her down in it, head first."

"Er, what about her hair? And that make up took me ages this morning. She'll end up a right mess. You can't ask her to do that, man."

"Look, just do it. Bernice will be here any minute and the headmaster as well."

"What?!" exclaimed me and Robbo together.

"Hang on, I can smell gas," I said.

"Yeah, that's the idea, dumbo," Gaz announced.

Rob and I gazed at each other then shrugged and got Flora down on the floor. I forced her head into the open oven.

"Sorry, pet," I told her. "Here, this gas isn't really on, is it?" I asked Gaz.

"No, but it has been, and Bernice won't know the difference, will she? As long as it smells like it is."

A pleasing little light of understanding was starting to flicker on in my brain.

"Oh, nice one, Gaz!" I laughed. Then, "Sorry, Flora, I'll just straighten your skirt for you. Don't want the whole world to see your Calvins as you gas yourself, do we?"

Gaz and I hid in a cupboard whilst Robbo went to wait outside of the door, a grubby hanky in his hands as he pretended to wipe his eyes with it.

Bernice's voice could be heard long before she hove into view.

"I mean it. If she's not here, we'll tear this place apart until we find her. Snotty cow, waving at me like that. I'll show her who she can wave at or not. Who does she think she is? The Queen?" She spotted Gaz then, blowing his nose into the hanky and breathing deeply.

"Oy, what's the matter with you, fish face? Is that new girl in there?"

"Oh, she's in there all right, but you can't go in," he sighed. "It's awful."

"I'll give you awful, Crater Face. Get outta my way, if you know what's good for you." She tried to push Gaz to one side. "I can smell a rat here. You're up to something. Where's that Will gone, her boyfriend?"

In the cupboard Rob and I began to giggle helplessly. I needed to go for a pee urgently but didn't dare go out yet. Next thing the door to the cookery room burst in and a bloodcurdling scream resounded around the room. Rob and I hung onto each other, eyes wide in disbelief, creased up with silent mirth.

"Oh my God! You stupid little slap…I mean, how could you, you silly little cow. I wasn't really going to hurt you! Come on, get up. You're not really dead, are you?"

I peeped from behind the cupboard door. Bernice was standing there, white as a sheet, her hair almost on end – though with all that gel it's hard to say really. Her eyes were out on stalks and she was gazing down on Flora with her head in the oven, but from a distance, as though she didn't dare go too close. She really did not want to confront this, knowing that she could be the cause. Bernice obviously believed that Flora had killed herself, and all because of her. The gang behind her had already legged it, leaving their leader to get herself out of the sticky stuff. Unknowingly, Gaz had slipped away to warn the headmaster of the situation. Meanwhile, in the cupboard, Rob and I were stuffing dishcloths into our mouths so we wouldn't scream out with laugher and give the game away. Our faces were bright red with the effort and our eyes were streaming.

"What the…? You, girl, do something useful. Ring for an ambulance immediately. And stop blubbering, you idiot!"

Blubbering! Blubber. Bernice. Oh no, this was almost too much for us to take.

Wahey – the heavy mob had arrived! It was the Head.

"You, boy, get help. Don't just stand there laughing. Help me to lift this girl. I'll get her legs and pull while you turn the gas off."

The next thing was me and Rob running out and mumbling to the headmaster through our dishcloths, but it was too late. By the time we got to him, he was sitting on the floor with one of Flora's legs in his hand. By now other staff had arrived and were gawping in disbelief, and Bernice was leaning over a bench, slobbering and gasping for air like a hippo in labour.

"I thought I'd killed her, sir," she managed to pant.

"So did I," the Head replied, gazing at the severed leg in his hand in a puzzled way. Then he spotted Robbo and me and his gaze seemed to snap into focus. "You two, my office, now."

By now I was cross-legged, jiggling with relief that we were all still in one piece but still desperately needing the bog. I was hanging on to my...well, you-know-whats, trying to keep it all in and the other hand was raised in the air like a six-year-old's.

"Sir, can I just... I really need to..." I stuttered.

"Now!" The Head roared.

Chapter 3

Our Head looks a bit like Peter Kay, only older, but he's not half as funny let me tell you. He eventually agreed that no-one had been seriously hurt or damaged, *this time, he said,* but he made us take Flora to the Drama department and put her in the store cupboard. I felt quite sick at the thought of leaving her there, stashed away with all those shrunken heads from the last production, and the three witches from Macbeth. I know us kids joked at the time that they were all previous teachers who had been caught out not marking exercise books on time, or those who were late for yard duty, but, in reality, they were quite scary. I didn't want Flora mixing with *those* sorts.

I was just about to nudge Gaz when the Head caught my eye and read my mind at the same time.

"And if you were thinking of NOT donating this dummy to the Drama department, Will Green, I am going to ask a member of staff on duty at home time to check that it really is in there. Securely locked away from silly little boys."

Damn! That's another plan down the bog.

We walked forlornly towards the Drama block, carrying Flora between us. Other kids passing sniggered and called out to us, trying to pat her bum or steal her wig. I tried to be calm. At least we were getting some kind of attention – SO much better than being ignored.

One of the year eleven goddesses, Fiona Bridges, passed us by, all long flowing blonde hair and perfume. We three dropped our eyes: we knew we could turn to stone just by gazing on her beauty.

"So, one of you pulled at last," she smiled and stopped us. "You must let me know who does her hair. It's so…" she tried to think of a suitable adjective "…grotty," Fiona decided.

Robbo stopped us and grinned at her, I was trying to look her in the eyes but found my gaze resting somewhere near the third button down on her blouse and Gaz was doing his constipated warthog face. Well – he was smiling, but Fiona wouldn't have realized that.

"Where are you taking this creature, then?" Fiona asked. "For an Italian meal? To the Pictures perhaps?"

Somehow Robbo found enough voice to explain our situation. We told Fiona how unhappy we were to lose the fabulous Flora and how we had planned to have a lot more fun with her but at that moment Mrs Hawkins, Hawkeye, came round the corner, her jam jar glasses gleaming.

"Now boys and girls," she announced, "the headmaster has asked me to check that you have put something important into the stock cupboard. Have you done that?"

Before I could answer, stupid Gaz replied, "Yes, Miss," and nodded at her.

"Good!" She smiled as Robbo and I looked daggers at him. Fiona simply raised her eyebrows elegantly. Flora, as you would expect, said nothing. "I'll be back in two minutes to have a look at exactly where you've put it so I can tell him you did as you were told." And she sailed off down the corridor.

I grabbed him by the collar. "You idiot! We could have made a run for it," I snarled.

Robbo, always cool in a situation, took hold of Fiona's hand.

"Please, Fiona, come into the Drama stock cupboard with me?" he begged. She laughed delightedly.

"You what?" she asked incredulously.

"Robbo, this is not the time for you to ..." I began but he interrupted me quickly.

"Shut up, Will. You three hide in that room behind the screen and leave me and Fiona to do what we have to do before Hawkeye comes back." Then he pushed me, Flora and Gaz into the medical room before dragging Fiona into the dark recesses of the Drama store cupboard.

"That boy's really got the hots for Fiona, or he's finally flipped," I told Gaz quietly. There was the sound of some muffled rustling and giggling. I was almost too embarrassed to look Gaz in the face, but the two of us were steaming.

"Jammy git," I hissed. Then the medical room door opened, and Robbo dragged out me and Gaz, back into the corridor.

"That was quick," I stated. "Where's F...?" I was stopped by the sudden return of Mrs Hawkins.

"Now then, boys, where's this awful dummy creature you've been messing about with all day?"

To our astonishment, Robbo calmly approached the door to the Drama store and opened it. Gaz and I looked at each other quizzically.

"There she is, Miss, down at the back, but you can't see very well from here cos the light's bust."

Really? I'm sure it was working a minute ago, when we decided we didn't want the fragrant Flora stashed in with all the smelly rubbish in there. At the back of the cupboard, I could dimly make out a female shape leaning up against the far wall. It was the same height and colouring as Flora, but I knew she was in the medical room, lying on the bed behind the screen. (Be still, my beating heart!)

"Not a problem, young man. I'll just step a bit closer. My eyes aren't as good as they once were, you know."

Oh oh, more trouble now, I thought.

"You go right ahead, Miss," Robbo told her as she started inside the long cupboard. I punched him on the shoulder in panic, but he continued. "Just watch you don't stand on any of those cute little baby mice though, Miss, will you? They can run ever so fast, but it is dark in there and you could have them running all over the school."

"Ah. Quite," came the teacher's strangled voice from out of the gloom. "Well, we wouldn't want that, would we? And I can see *quite* clearly from here that that hideous creature is back where she belongs. I'll tell the Head that you did as you were told. Well done, boys," and she was away down the corridor as fast as her fat little cellulite legs would carry her.

"Phew! That was close!" I breathed. "Where did Fiona get to?" I asked Robbo.

A voice from back of the cupboard stated: "The hideous creature is in here!" And she emerged into the corridor to join us, shaking dust and cobwebs from her hair and smiling like the Mona Lisa. God, but she was gorgeous.

We all started laughing together then. We introduced Fiona to Flora properly and decided to make our escape while the going was good. Robbo took hold of Fiona's hand and kissed her on her soft cheek.

"Thanks, Fiona. You're a star!" he told her. Gaz and I were struck dumb as we left the school and crossed the yard hurriedly before anyone else could stop us.

Gaz was the first one to interrupt our thoughts.

"God, that was close. I can't believe she did that. She's really something, eh?"

"Amazing," I agreed, imagining those blue eyes homing in for a kiss. I could even feel myself beginning to pucker up.

"Watch it, you two, you'll make Flora jealous," Robbo told us, jostling her into a more comfortable position between us.

"Oh, Flora's a bit better than her, don't you think?" Gaz asked.

Rob and I looked at him, then at Flora, and then back at Gaz. Now, I knew he quite fancied Flora but really, compared to the real thing? I mean... *Fiona Bridges*?

"So, you fancy going out with her then? Don't let us two stand in your way, Gaz. This could be the start of a wonderful relationship."

"Yuk! Are you mad?" he demanded.

By now we had all stopped and were becoming confused. Gaz has that effect on some people.

"Why would I want to go out with Mrs Hawkins?" he asked, shaking his head. Now it was our turn.

"Mrs Hawkins? You fancy *Mrs Hawkins*?" Rob asked, but I had got the message.

"Oh, look, he thought we meant…that we were talking about… oh, never mind. It'll take too long, and we could be old men before the penny drops for this one. Let's get Flora home. Mrs Hawkins indeed! Leave me to dream about the wonderful Fiona." But I couldn't help staring at Rob and wondering about that kiss on the cheek.

We joined the High Street and slowed down a bit. I couldn't help but continue to stare at Robbo though. He caught me looking.

"What?" he asked.

"Well, you know when you and Fiona were in the stock cupboard?" I began.

"Yeah?" He smiled again, that self-satisfied, smug smile.

"Did you feel yourself turning to stone?" I asked him, grinning back. Gaz just looked puzzled, and then Rob winked at me.

"It was very hard… not to," he announced with a laugh.

"You what? What are you on about?" Gaz demanded.

I ruffled his hair.

"I'll tell you when you're a big boy!" And Rob and I laughed out loud.

We ambled on, talking about what we could get up to that night that didn't cost more than three pounds twenty-four pence, which is how much we had together, when suddenly I was lifted bodily off the ground and pinned up against the wall behind the old cinema. I shut my eyes and choked, fighting for breath. Someone or something had me in a grip like King Kong. The foul breath told me it *was* King Kong

– well, Bernice anyway. Gingerly I opened one eye. She was holding me level with her face.

"Gotcha, you little maggot!"

"Strewth, Bernice, you're stronger than you look," I managed to gasp with great difficulty; she was choking me half to death. My shirt, jumper and blazer were gripped in her huge meaty hand and I could feel my trousers starting to part company with my waist. I managed to block out a terrifying vision of me hanging there in mid-air, feet dangling and other bits dangling too. I prayed I was wearing my Calvins and not the y-fronts my Nan had got me last Christmas.

"You think you're so flaming clever, don't you? You and your grungy little mates."

Grungy? Us? Now that was unfair, especially coming from someone who looked and smelled, walked and talked like an extra from the Star Wars bar.

"Well, this time you've gone too far, you little rat. I've had about enough of you making me a laughing stock."

She had gradually lowered me to the ground, but her hold was still like a vice. I felt my knees knocking. I knew she wouldn't be alone. Her gang would be hiding under a stone or behind a bin or somewhere. I could hear Gaz and Robbo making general protestations, but they were totally ineffective against an enemy this size. I began to mentally make a general list of who should inherit my belongings, like men on death row must do, when –*Thank You, God*– a police patrol car came around the corner! Bernice saw it and gave me one huge shove which sent me sprawling backwards onto the pavement. I bashed the back of my head and lay there seeing stars for a minute. She sauntered off, giving the two officers in the car a cheery wave and blew them a kiss. They don't pay those guys enough, I can tell you.

The lads helped me up.

"Are you ok, mate?" Rob asked, gently straightening my shirt and blazer.

Gaz was standing with half a brick in one hand. I gave him a quizzical look.

"I would have used it," he declared. "Bitch!"

"Thanks, Pal, but I fear it would have been like chucking a cherry stone at the Empire State Building."

"Come on, let's get out of here before she comes back to finish us off." Rob made a move for home, and I was relieved to limp along between my two mates and a slightly shocked Flora.

We discussed whether it was still worth going out that night. We had hardly any dosh; I was battered and bruised so we needed to make plans carefully. Gaz was still fuming about Bernice, but Rob and I tried to pacify him.

"One day we'll laugh at this," I told Gaz, gingerly rubbing my bruised throat. "When she's a sad, pathetic lonely spinster we three will be having the last laugh. We'll tell our stunning girlfriends how we were once stalked by a crazed she-devil and lived to tell the tale."

Rob's eyes seemed to light up a little and he quickened his pace.

"Yes, but, she's not lonely, is she?" sighed Gaz.

"Her gang of deadheads won't stay with her forever," I said. "Before you know it, they'll have been caught in some rays of sunshine and been vapourised, or end up in Borstal or somewhere."

"No, I mean her and Mad Mick are an item. They've been going out. With each other," he added, for dramatic effect.

The four of us stopped in our tracks. Robbo and I looked at Gaz in puzzlement.

"Have you been at your mam's nail varnish remover again, Gaz?" I asked patiently.

"Honest, it's true," he replied, nodding his head frantically. "I saw them with my very own eyes. Last Friday night when I went to the chippy. They were kissing and slobbering all over each other in the bus stop. Nearly put me off my cheesy chips! Every Friday night he sneaks Bernice into his shed in the rail yard. I thought you knew. I thought everybody knew that."

"Yuk, gross!" Rob looked like he was going to throw up but I, on the other hand, was forming a plan.

"Oh lads, this could be where we get our own back. Broadwalk and Mad Mick together. We're going to have some fun!"

"What? What are you thinking of doing, Will?" asked Rob in a cautious voice.

"Well, we've got to plan this carefully. You, me, Gaz and one of the dummies, in the rail yard. Come on, it'll be a right laugh. You know how Mad Mick hates us and how easy he is to wind up. We can torment the life out of him. He might even get the sack, then how would he keep the beautiful Bernice in hair gel and liver sandwiches? We can kill two birds with one stone!"

The lads were beginning to pick up by then and were obviously forming ideas of their own.

"This has to be planned right down to the final detail, mind you," Rob said. "We can't leave anything to chance."

We stood together in the middle of the street, grinning inanely at each other in wonderment.

"Board room, tonight, lads. What time?" I asked.

"I want to watch Coronation..." Gaz began, but me and Rob jumped on him.

***

Our garden shed used to be a tidy little haven, where me and Ross stashed stuff we didn't want Jilly to get her paws on, and where we could hide when it was our turn to do the washing up. It was a warm, cosy little spot, tucked away right in the bottom corner of the garden. There were raspberry canes and nettles in front of it, an overgrown pond that attracted newts, toads and frogs, and because those particular forms of wildlife would see Mam and Jilly running screaming for the hills, we were rarely interrupted in there. And now, of course, I was the only person ever to visit.

Coming into the shed always gave me a feeling of guilt, wrapped around with reverence, peace and comfort. The light fell gently through the dusty window panes, dust motes floated, gentle and golden in the still air. There was a stash of old comics, some bottles of pop hidden away, the odd dirty magazine from yonks back, and a dartboard on the wall. A couple of ancient chairs with the stuffing spilling out made it seem like a little bit of heaven, especially when the storm lamp was lit in the evenings and the rain was coming down softly on the tin roof. Ross and I spent many a happy hour in there, hiding from housework duties, telling rude jokes and not doing our homework. Even though he was so much older than me, Ross treated me like his best mate, his buddy, not his snotty-nosed kid brother.

I checked the coast was clear and sneaked past the kitchen window to the shed. I had already made sure the dummies were safely hidden in my bedroom; I wanted to tell Ross about the fun we had already had with them and was chuckling to myself as the door creaked open. Peering into the gloom, I made my way to the back of the shed, avoiding the lawnmower and some old tins of paint. Finding my way carefully, I soon felt the little candles I had "borrowed" from St Peter's Church and the box of matches tucked away behind a bag of cement. Lighting them carefully, almost reverently, I stood back and smiled.

The photo of Ross was one that had been taken when he made a whole-school presentation as Head Boy. He was standing behind the lectern on our stage, smiling confidently at someone in the back of the hall, probably me. Tall, dark, handsome *and* clever, our Ross was the real deal. He had a wicked sense of humour, and I just knew he'd love the dummies and our antics. I could feel him encouraging me on, laughing with me and the lads, and telling Jilly to just chill and enjoy the fun.

The little candles threw off a subtle light onto Ross's photo, casting warm shadows around the dimly lit shed. It really did remind me of being in church; he appeared to have a halo. *Not wrong there,* I thought. I shuddered a bit at the thought of the last time I had been in a church, giving my head a shake and pulling up an old chair in front of the photo. I smiled shyly up at the image of my brother, my mate, my best friend.

"Ross," I began. "Wait till I tell you what us lads have been getting up to. You're going to love this."

I settled in for my regular weekly chat with my big bro, warming to the theme, and appreciating his friendly, encouraging smile.

Chapter 4

It was a bit squashed in my bedroom with the six of us – me, Gaz, Robbo, Flora, Keith and a very naked Nigel. Us lads were actually a bit embarrassed about the fact that Nigel had been left out of the proceedings so far, so we put my pyjama bottoms on him and sat him at my desk with a pen in one hand, so he could make notes for us and act as secretary for the meeting. I thought he had been looking quite forlorn, but he cheered up a bit after that. Flora was sitting on my bed and Keith was lying half in and half out of my wardrobe. I had tried to stand him in there properly, but he broke the wooden fort that I was keeping for a special occasion, then my collection of priceless glass marbles fell on top of him, so I gave up and just stuffed him in the bottom, head first.

"That's hardly dignified, is it?" Rob asked.

"It's his fault. He broke my fort. He should have watched where he was putting his big feet," I told him. "He better not have broken my marbles," I continued, putting them back into the sweet tin where they rattled about comfortingly.

"Why DO they call them marbles, anyway?" Gaz asked. "They aren't made of marble, are they?"

"It's dark in there," Rob replied, ignoring Gaz and coming to Nigel's defence. "He can't see what he's doing. And anyway, your wardrobe is a tip. You want to get it tidied up a bit."

I hit him with my pillow then. "You sound just like my mam," I told him. "Now, can we bring this meeting to order?"

"Ok, boss," Rob nodded.

"Certainly," Gaz stated.

"Right then, let's begin with..."

"Er, haven't you forgotten something?" Gaz asked.

"What? I always ask the members if we're ready," I told him.

In reply, Gaz simply raised his eyebrows and nodded in the direction of the dummies.

I sighed. "What now?" I asked wearily.

"You didn't ask them if they were ready."

Rob exploded.

"Gaz, man, give over. Can we just get on with the meeting?"

Gaz moved a little closer towards Flora on the bed. I swear he was holding her hand at one point.

"Fair's fair, now, lads. They have to be sworn in if they are going to be part of our gang. After all, we've become quite close to them in the last couple of days."

I couldn't believe what I was hearing.

"That's total crap," I started, but Gaz jumped in.

"Sshh!" he said, holding his hands over Flora's ears. "That's not the sort of swearing I meant," he hissed.

Rob started to laugh.

"Oh, for f... Pete's sake," he began, looking closely at Flora. "Let's just get on with it."

I stood up with resignation and sighed dramatically.

"Right then. As founder member" (giggle from Gaz) "of this, the SGA association, I hereby declare that Flora, Keith and Nigel are now fully fledged members of the aforementioned gang." I sat down again, on the floor.

"Remind me about why we called ourselves the SGA again," Rob said.

"Sad Gits Association," I told him bluntly. "Because none of us has ever had a girlfriend or come anywhere close to finding one. Now, can we get on please?"

Finally, we discussed the various number of entertaining and highly impractical ways we could think of for ridding the world of the burden that was Bernice. Short of boiling her in oil, disembowelling her and packing her off to Peru in little bundles, we didn't really have a clue. Rob thought we could entice her to a high cliff top and throw a couple of Mars bars over for her to chase, like a dog after a stick, but we decided against it on the grounds of safety – for whoever may be unlucky enough to be sitting underneath. Gaz was in the process of explaining a complicated plan which involved constructing a giant catapult, made from Bernice's very own knicker elastic and a large tarpaulin, when the door burst open. Jilly, of course. She stood there gazing about the room disdainfully for a second as I demanded:

"Jilly, can't you ever knock?"

"No, actually," she replied, "not with these nails on."

Her lips pursed as she surveyed my bedroom, which I must admit was a bit of a dump by then. Keith was back out of the wardrobe and Nigel was slumped forward over the desk, his wig over one eye, the other one seemingly gazing at Jilly. On the bed, Rob had placed one arm protectively around Flora's shoulders. She was still wearing her school uniform and was sort of leaning forward into him. I thought they looked rather sweet together actually.

"What do you want, anyway?" I asked my annoying big sister.

"You know, I really don't understand why you three hang around with these pale faced, miserable weirdoes," she stated, looking around the room.

Rob took exception to that.

"Oy, watch it, you'll upset the dummies," he exclaimed.

"I was talking to the dummies," she replied with a smirk.

"Oh, ha bloody ha," I announced, sarcastically. "Tell us what you want, witch, then sod off out of here."

"Mam says have you done the homework yet?" she sneered, knowing fine well that it would wipe the smiles off our faces.

"Which homework?" I asked, looking to my friends for assistance on this one. They looked back blankly, shrugging their shoulders.

"The one you got a detention for not doing last week," she reminded us. "It's due in tomorrow, Mam says. She thinks that, as it's a group activity, that's what you are trying to do in here. Mind you, I could tell her that you three are up to no good again, you saddos."

When we still looked back at her vacantly, open mouthed in Gaz's case, she told us triumphantly, "Citizenship? You apparently have to have a four-week action plan in by tomorrow? If not, you three will be grounded, oh, for...well, for EVER I would say!"

The penny dropped with some force then, I can assure you. I clamped my hands over my face, eyes wide in horror, Rob slid off the chair he'd been sitting on and started swearing loudly and Gaz started to laugh, or cry – it's not always easy to tell with him. From downstairs I could hear my mam's voice shouting up with some menace.

"William, stop that vulgar swearing and get on with your homework!"

I was up and had my hands clamped tightly over Rob's nose and mouth by then.

"Sorry, Mam. We're nearly finished now," I called back downstairs. The lads were silent in disbelief. Jilly still had that smirk on her painted face. She needed such a slap, that girl. She sneered down at us.

"You've got five minutes before I..." she began, then she looked at Gaz sitting there on the bed beside Flora and gasped, "oh, you, you... pervert!" before going bright red and slamming the door with a flourish. We could hear her storming into the kitchen, wailing "Mam, you'll never believe what those three are playing at..." before her voice was drowned out by Rob's hysterical laughter.

"What?" I demanded, looking about the room for clues as to what had so upset Jilly and what had so entertained Rob. Gaz looked from each of us, as nonplussed as I was. He shook his head.

"It wasn't me," he whined. "I haven't done anything wrong. What did she want to go and call me that for then?"

But then I saw it too, and it just about finished me off as well. Rob and I held on to each other and danced up and down in glee as we realized what Jilly had been going on about. Flora had fallen forwards and sideways when Gaz had shifted on the bed and now her face, or more accurately her mouth, was lying in Gaz's lap and one of her hands was buried in his crotch. At that point he looked down and realized what it must have looked like. He too began to giggle, then laugh out loud, then roar with laughter along with us two, whilst I got my mobile phone out and we spent a very silly five minutes, photographing Gaz and Flora in compromising positions, until my mam had had enough and told Rob and Gaz to get out.

"What about the Citizenship homework though?" Rob asked. "Another detention and I'm off the football team. We'll have to think of something quick!"

"What did we have to do, anyway?" Gaz asked as I frantically searched through my desk drawers for the assignment title.

"Oh no. We had to plan and explain a community-based project which us three could carry out over a couple of weeks. We're stuffed. Mr Angus will have us shot if we don't come up with something really catchy and entertaining. He's bringing the local paper in and everything on this one."

"Oh b...*binoculars!*" Rob declared, remembering my mam downstairs. "Isn't that the homework that snotty little Karen Greg is planning to decorate an old lady's house or something?"

"The very same," I told him. "And Mark Baxter's group are going to clear all the rubbish out of the stream in the park for their project. If we don't come up with something equally good and rewarding, we're knacked!"

I looked at Gaz, still sitting next to Flora on the bed, but decently now that he had sat her back up again. He seemed to be quite red in the face though, like a baby straining to fill its nappy.

"Gaz, are you all right, mate?" I asked him.

"Yeah, I'm just trying to, you know, think of a really good idea for this," he told me.

Gaz and I looked at each other and smiled.

"Yeah, right," I stated. "Let me know as soon as one comes in."

"Or out..." Rob laughed.

Then Jilly came back in and threw us all out, so we didn't have time to plan to either kill off Bernice or decide on a good enough excuse for not coming up with yet another homework for Citizenship. Oh, woe is me!

As the lads slouched out through the front gate, I called down to them from my bedroom window,

"The first person to come up with a really good idea has to phone the rest of us with it. The winner gets to snog Fiona Bridges in the Drama store cupboard! OK?"

In the garden below, I laughed as my two mates grinned back at me and slapped the air between them in a high five salute. The last thing I heard as I pulled the window shut was our Jilly's voice calling back to them.

"Shut the gate after you. Perverts!"

I went back to my bed and sat down beside a rather dishevelled Flora.

"Eeh, what a woman." I smiled to myself.

Chapter 5

At 2.15 in the morning my mobile bleeped. It was a message from Rob. It read: *"Sorted! Got just the job for our project. us 3 r adopting J J. c u tomorra n I'll explain."*

It meant nothing to me at that time of the night but I had enough confidence in my oldest, most trusted mate so I quickly settled down to sleep again. Now, if that text had come from Gaz, I'd have been having nightmares all night.

We met next morning, as usual, on the railway bridge to make our way to school together. It was a bright sunny morning and as Rob had got there early, he felt it had been his proud duty to get some target practice in on Mad Mick, as he came out of his security hut after a night patrolling the railyards and sidings. Rob laughed as he explained how he had picked up a handful of pinecones and had spent a happy ten minutes pinging them off Mick's windows, then at his head, as he came out to investigate the noises. Rob is slim and fast, far too quick for the likes of bulky, sulky Mad Mick, and he kept ducking down behind the parapet of the bridge every time Mick peered up at him. By the time Gaz and I joined him, we could hear the rage in Mick's voice as he bellowed from down below.

"I know you three. You sad little shysters! I'll get you one day. You just watch your backs. You're like three-year-olds, only without their intelligence. If I catch up with you, I'll rip your faces off! Now piss off to school before I set the dog on you."

Well, that was just too good an opportunity to miss. No self-respecting teenage boy could walk away from a challenge like that one.

"The dog?" I yelled back. "She'll just be scoffing her morning Mars Bar by now. Oh, you mean the *guard* dog!"

We ran, falling over ourselves in delight at having started his day so badly. We went into Bal's shop for a snack, coming out with a custard slice, a cheese pasty and a can of fizzy blue pop. I looked at Gaz who was slouching along, stuffing the pasty into his mouth. He looked a bit pale and undernourished, with his cap on backwards, but that was nothing unusual for Gaz.

"You not buying any chewy then, Gaz?" I asked. He always bought a packet every morning. It was his ritual. He looked a bit sheepish but shook his head, mumbling something unintelligible, but that was a ritual for him too, so I thought nothing more of it. As we approached the school gates, the teachers on duty started harassing us with their usual daily routine.

"Morning, chaps. Tuck your shirts in, take your hats off inside please and make sure you've got your blazers on."

Ignoring them, as usual, I asked Rob about our Citizenship homework. His face lit up.

"Oh lads, wait till I tell you. It's a brilliant plan. You'll love it, we'll have a laugh doing it and we might even get our photos in the local paper!"

"Come on then, spill the beans. We need to know now. We've got Citizenship first lesson," I urged him. Our form tutor was coming down the stairs by then and spotted us.

"Good heavens, you three, on time. What happened? Have you not been home since last night?"

Oh, she thinks she's such a wit, that one.

"Ha ha, Miss. Much as we'd love to spend *every* evening in detention with you, we do have other lives and interests, you know," Rob told her with a smile. He has the sort of face which can get away with talking to a teacher like that. I'd be permanently excluded if I tried it and Gaz would just get a slap.

"Morning, Miss." Gaz smiled at her.

"Get your hat off, Gordon," she replied, walking away. Normally he would have ripped it off his head and stuffed it into his pocket. Today I watched, puzzled, as he pretended to do that but dropped his hand from his cap as soon as the teacher was out of sight. Oh well.

"Come on, Rob; tell us so we can at least *look* as though we planned the whole thing together." I was beginning to worry now as the time to go to lesson one was fast approaching, and I really didn't need another detention. His reply was cut off by the buzzer to start the day. I sighed and followed him into the classroom, hanging back to catch a glimpse of Fiona Bridges swinging along the corridor ahead of me. Oh bliss!

Mr Angus was late, as ever, so we did all the usual stuff like seeing who could crawl around the whole room the fastest on top of all the tables, without ever touching the floor with your hands or feet. Then we started playing body-parts-hangman on the board and little Stu decided to hide inside the filing cabinet cupboard so we put a bookcase in front of it. Well, the lock was broken. The girls just sat discussing who had snogged who last night and gave us withering looks, whilst pretending they really weren't interested in us. Actually, they weren't at all. To them, we were only one step up from amoeba. Soon we were bored and scrambled to our seats as Mr Angus burst into the room in a bit of a state.

"You lot should have been ready ages ago, sitting in your OWN places and with all the books out. Now get organized, quick. It's bad enough being held up with a fight in the Art block without coming in to this chaos." He proceeded to do the register for that lesson. I still didn't know what our project was going to be, but didn't panic because Rob can generally charm his way out of most situations. If he said we were sorted, then I had nothing to worry about.

"Karen Clark?"

"Sir."

"Nick Davies?"

'Sir."

"Gordon Freeman?"

"Sir," Gaz replied, and the teacher told him, without even looking up from the computer, "Take that cap off, Gordon."

Again, Gaz ignored the command. By now Rob and I were beginning to wonder about this. We looked at each other in a bemused way and shook our heads. Gaz was quite pink. Something was up.

The time soon came for everyone to explain their action plan for the community-based project. Oh well, Rob my son, it's now or never, I thought.

"And now it's your turn. Which one of you bright sparks is going to tell us about your wonderful ideas?" Mr Angus asked, looking as though he knew full well it would probably be a pile of poo, if we actually *had* an idea in the first place. Rob sat up straighter in his seat, cleared his throat theatrically and began with an expansive smile.

"Ah now, sir, what we thought was…." But the teacher cut in with:

"Gordon. How many times have you been told to get that hat off in school? Remove it, now!"

Rob tutted in exasperation and glared at Gaz.

"Gaz, man, just get on with it, will you? This is our big moment," he hissed. Gaz looked uncomfortable and began mumbling something about having a headache and that keeping his cap on helped. The teacher was starting to really lose it, so I reached over and grabbed the cap myself. I quickly stuffed it in my pocket and nodded to Rob to continue with the explanation. He had just opened his mouth when some of the girls behind us started giggling and pointing to the back of Gaz's head. Then some of the lads joined in too.

"Oh, for God's sake, now what?!" Mr Angus demanded. At that point Gaz turned round in his seat to swear at the girls and we too began to laugh then: stuck in the back of his hair were ribbons of chewing gum, hanging almost from ear to ear like a string of pearls.

"Ah, Gaz! What are you playing at, man? That stinks for a start!"

Mr Angus took control quickly. "Gordon, how can you come to school like that? Come here so I can have a proper look."

Gaz shuffled out of his seat and moved to the front of the class, taking swipes at whoever was daft enough to make a snide comment.

"My mam said I had to come in like this, sir," he told the teacher. "She said it was punishment for falling asleep with chewy in my mouth. It must have fallen out when I was asleep and now it's all stuck everywhere. I couldn't see the back of my own head to cut it out, and I knew everyone would laugh so I was just going to wear my cap all day, until I could get to the barbers, like, after school."

He was a sorry sight, I have to admit. Mr Angus inspected the back of Gaz's head, curling his lip in distaste as he reached into his drawer for some large scissors. Everyone in the room gasped, dramatically.

"Oh, shut up you lot," Mr Angus told them, with a scary sort of smile. We watched, everyone all agoggle, as Mr Angus hacked off chunks of Gaz's hair. The boys cheered with every snip and the girls stifled screams and hid their eyes as clumps of hair fell to the floor. When the last bits were in the bin, Gaz almost swaggered back to his seat and Rob tried again.

"Right, sir. What we thought we'd do was..."

The teacher held up a hand.

"So sorry to stop you once again, Robert, but what *is* that noise?"

Everyone stopped to listen, eyes floating around the room looking for the source of a peculiar squeaking.

"Oh, that'll be the sound of Sam's brain clanking into gear."

Someone laughed.

Sam was not amused. She flounced back her long curls and retorted, "Shut your face, ape man. At least my brains aren't in my arse!"

The teacher was losing patience and so was I, actually. Here we were, 25 minutes into the lesson, and I still didn't know our grand plan. No-one seemed to know what the sound was or where it was coming from.

Mr Angus started pacing the room, listening in carefully to locate the source of the sound. As he approached the bookcase he asked, "What is this doing here? It's supposed to be..." Then he stopped, glared around the room and roughly dragged the bookcase away from the filing cupboard. He wrenched open the door and out fell a gasping Little Stu, all sweaty and laughing in relief, until he saw the look on Mr Angus' face. This was followed by howls of approval or disbelief by those who had actually forgotten Stu was in the cupboard. I know I had. So then we were all made to stand outside in the corridor while Mr Angus ranted and raved about our juvenile, dangerous stupidity before we were marched back in to sit alphabetically boy/girl. D'oh!

"Now, finally Robert, and believe me it had better be good after all that. Explain what you, Will and Gordon will be doing for your community-based project."

Rob stood up and began. Gaz and I watched, fascinated.

"Right, sir. If I may continue, WITHOUT INTERRUPTION–" he glared at the class who waited eagerly.

"There is a tramp who..."

"A what?" asked Mr Angus, one eyebrow raised in question.

"A homeless man," Rob corrected himself, "known locally as Jimmy Jesus," he said, casting withering looks at the kids who giggled at the sound of the name. "Well, we have decided to adopt him, so to speak."

At this, the class roared in disbelief. Everyone in the area knew of Jimmy Jesus. Rob's idea was just a bit too off the wall, even for me. I looked at him as if he was mad. So did Mr Angus.

"So, you want to adopt this tramp...er...homeless person, and do ...what exactly?" he asked us.

"Bath him, for a start!" someone shouted from the back, to everyone's great amusement.

"Well, yes, to begin with," Rob confirmed. I was warming to the theme now. I could see where we were going with this if no-one else could.

"Then get him some new clothes, a haircut…" Gaz added, pointing self-consciously to his own head.

"And try to find him somewhere to live," I concluded. We three sat back then and waited for a reaction. Mr Angus stared at us very carefully to see if we were taking the mick.

"Well," he declared, "that's not at all what I was expecting from you three. It's a bit rough around the edges, but with a LOT of thought and some careful consideration we may be on to something here."

He rubbed his chin thoughtfully for a moment and seemed to go off into some imaginary world. He was probably seeing the headlines in the local rag, something like "*Tramp Saved by Teen Heroes*". Or, "*Jimmy Jesus, Born Again*".

I gazed in hero worship at my mate Rob. What a star this lad is! I thought. This was a project we could really get our teeth into and get some good from at the same time. Oh yes, this was one lesson we would have some fun in and save Rob's place on his beloved school footy team. The possibilities were endless.

I glanced around. Some of the other pupils were watching us warily, some with obvious jealousy for not coming up with such a classic idea, and others were quite simply mocking us. One or two whispers could be heard, comments like:

"Do they really think Jimmy will let them three do anything for him?"

"They're mad! They'll catch something awful off Jimmy."

But by then I didn't care. I had this vision of us three standing having our photos taken for The Echo with Jimmy standing beside us, hair cut, shaved, wearing a smart suit and shoes and looking quite plump and healthy. We were all beaming with pride. Eeh, I've always wanted to be in the Echo!

In my daydream, my parents were there as well, beaming, because I had finally achieved something worthy in my life. Our Ross had always been the family hero, not me, so for once I was the centre of attention – and all for the *right* reasons for a change. I was just about to drift into the dreamy scenario of some girls coming to us to ask our advice on their own projects. My eyes were beginning to glaze over, my jaw to become slack when I was rudely awoken by a dig from Rob.

Next thing the buzzer sounded, and we all trooped off to Maths.

Mr Angus called after us. "Well done, you three. We'll have to get together to discuss this with the headmaster."

For once, life in school felt good at that moment, but of course, there's a fly in every ointment and our own particular fly buzzed into action without warning. Bernice.

Chapter 6

The first I knew about it was when my face was roughly pushed into the wall down the corridor from our Citizenship lesson and a voice like a chainsaw whined in my ear.

"Mick tells me you three have been winding him up again."

Oh, great. Me versus the Minotaur, again.

"Look, Bernice, it wasn't us this time. We *like* Mick. We think he does a great job there in the yard."

Kids were starting to crowd round, watching in case there was going to be a barney, but where were my cavalry when I needed them? Just then I heard Gaz's voice. Oh, thanks, mate. Help was at hand, which was just as well cos there was never a teacher on duty when you needed one.

"Nah," Gaz was sneering, "it wasn't us, Bernice."

The grip on the back of my head was loosening slightly. Did she actually believe him? Now that WOULD be a first, but then thicko Gaz continued.

"Nah, we wouldn't throw pinecones at Mick's head. We'd throw bricks and do the job properly!"

Well, I thought my nose was about to burst all down the magnolia walls then as the grip on my head tightened once more. There was a general pushing and shoving all around me. I didn't know if it was Bernice and her henchmen (hench-women?) moving in for the kill, or the kids around us just urging us on into more action, but the next thing was Mr Angus bellowing down the corridor,

"Pack it in, you lot, and get to your next lesson. Now!"

With one final twist of my nose into the wall Bernice let go and started to wander off, but not before reaching into my pocket and grabbing Gaz's cap. She waved it triumphantly in my face and thrust it up inside her blouse where it bulged out like a gross third boob.

"Come and have a go, if you think you're HARD enough," she sang. Well, I say sang, but in actual fact it sounded more like the mating call of a moose. Like, I would even want to *go* there! I shuddered and backed off, smiling grimly to myself. It wasn't even my cap, and it stank of ancient chewy, but of course, she didn't know that. Bernice now had a trophy to take back to her beloved Mick, so she sailed off happily down the corridor, surrounded by her motley crew of munchkins.

I held a piece of grotty tissue to my nose that someone had thrust into my hand and looked round for the lads. And, whoah! Who should be standing there, offering sympathetic glances, but the beautiful Fiona Bridges? It was almost worth having my face mangled for a close encounter of this kind.

"Are you ok, Will?" she asked, frowning slightly. Two of her friends were with her, both pretty good-looking too, but I was blinded by her beauty and close proximity. I started to sweat and shake. *Oh, get a grip lad. Have a word with yourself,* I thought. But in the next nanosecond I thought, *no, don't hang on, Will. Go on, faint. Right into her arms. Then she can give me the kiss of life!* I started to slide down the wall.

I must have looked like such a drip, but then I heard Robbo saying, "You know, you'd think he'd be satisfied with ONE Florence Nightingale, but three? It's alright, ladies. We'll take over from here. Let's go and get this face of yours seen to, mate." And he grabbed me under the arms and almost bodily lifted me away, down towards the boy's bogs.

I was beginning to smile to myself – painfully – when I heard Gaz telling the girls, "We've been trying to get his face seen to for years. He still looks ugly!"

Aye, well, that's what friends are for.

***

Back in the boardroom we began hatching our plan to rescue Jimmy Jesus from his humdrum, monotonous and stinky life. For once Flora, Nigel and Keith were of secondary importance, but we explained to them very carefully that they just had to regard this as a little break. A holiday, perhaps. When the time was right, they would be out and about with us once again, putting on the style and making merriment to brighten up the dull routine of our lives. Causing chaos might have been a better way to put it, but we didn't want to worry them. We decided that Rob would be the secretary this time, rather than Nigel, because Rob was a quicker writer. Gaz pointed out that Nigel could probably spell better than Rob, but we knew that only Rob could read his own handwriting and as the whole thing was his idea, he would be the chosen one to type it all up and present it to Mr Angus. Hey, there's one born every minute, isn't there?

"Do you think that's fair?" Rob asked in a puzzled sort of way.

"Strewth, yes," I told him. "You deserve all the credit for this idea, mate. You don't want me and Gaz to mess it up now, do you?" I winked at Gaz. "I mean, we're just the action men. We're here to support you in every way we can."

He still didn't seem convinced, so we talked in detail about how we were going to approach Jimmy.

"Why do they call him Jimmy Jesus, anyway?" Gaz asked.

"I suppose it's the long hair, beard and long coat that gives the game away," I replied, sarcastically.

"Maybe he does miracles," Gaz replied.

Rob laughed. "Well, he performed one today."

We sat up, shocked.

"Honest? What did he do?" I asked in awe.

"He got us out of detention, didn't he, and kept me on the footy team," Rob laughed. "And he's always got a bottle wrapped up in a brown bag, yet he's got no money. So, maybe he turns water into wine as well!"

Gaz seemed to be taking this too seriously: I watched him nodding his head and chewing his gum rather too thoughtfully.

"Joke, Gaz," I warned him. "Rob's taking the mickey."

Gaz focused in on me then.

"He's got my cap," he stated.

"Who? Jimmy Jesus?" Rob asked, puzzled.

"No. Mick, Mad Mick. Bernice took my cap and passed it on to Mick. I want it back."

We sighed in unison, Rob and me.

"Look, forget about those two for now. This is far more interesting, and far less dangerous," I told him.

"What, persuading a psychotic old alcoholic to get a bath, eat something and wear real clothes and deodorant is less dangerous than Mick and Bernice? I don't think so."

Rob laughed. "Oh, don't lose heart. I would say the risk is halfy-half. Think of the glory we'll get… I mean, think how much good we'll be doing, saving Jimmy from yet another winter on those mean streets."

"Here, he lives near me, and my street isn't that mean," Gaz retorted.

"Lads, lads," I jumped in. "This is getting us nowhere. Now come on. We need to plan how we'll get Jimmy to come in for a bath and something to eat first."

There followed a seriously long discussion about whose house we would use to make our first assault on the scruffy Jimmy, but first what we could use as bait to catch him. Pies, whisky and our Jilly were all mentioned, but we thought we'd settle on waving a fiver under his nose if he wouldn't come quietly. Gaz said he knew where there was a big net, just in case things got a bit tricky, and Rob suggested we use some of Keith's clothes to replace the stinking rags Jimmy had worn for phew, well, the last five years that we knew him.

"Let me get this right," I began slowly. "First of all, we catch our tramp, bring him home, STRIP HIM, put him in a bath, feed him with Rob's mam's best steak and kidney pudding, then dress him up as a year nine pupil? He's about 60, for God's sake!"

Rob started to laugh.

Gaz looked at me like I'd finally cracked. "Eh?" he asked.

I patiently explained that when we took Keith into school, we dressed him as a pupil so as not to cause too big a disturbance.

"Oh, right, I'm with you now, Will," he laughed.

So, we had decided that we needed some proper warm clothing when Gaz offered his old Nike bottoms with rip off strips and a Burberry jumper.

"Gaz, mate, that's really sweet of you but this guy is at least 60. We need the sort of stuff our grandads would wear, not something he's going to go bopping about in a club in,"

Rob explained.

"The whole purpose of this scheme is to turn Jimmy into something acceptable to decent society, not into an advert for "Chavs-are-us."

But by then I was laughing at the thought of Jimmy Jesus, long hair flying, wearing untied trainers, a cap on backwards, his trackie bottoms tucked into his socks and one of those hideous gold clowns dancing around his dirty, scrawny neck. We were all rolling around and being incredibly silly when the door opened and there stood Jilly, watching us as if we were something she had trod in.

"I thought you three would still be in detention for not doing your homework assignment," she sneered.

"Jilly, it's half past eight," Rob told her.

"Exactly," she replied. "Don't tell me you actually came up with a proposal."

I glared at the other two to not say a word: I didn't want the wicked witch of the west putting a hex on our plans. Rob leaned forward towards her eagerly.

"Ah, we have, and you might be just the person to help us with a little problem we're having, Jilly."

She watched him suspiciously through the half open door. I noticed that Jilly never came fully into my room when the lads were in there with me.

"What?" she asked in sullen suspicion.

"Well, we need to pick up a strange old man from down near the docks and bring him back here, so we thought we'd ask you for some tips," Rob told her seriously.

Her face went white, then pink, then she leaned into the room as far as she dared and glowered at us.

"Oh, you…you…Perverts!"

She slammed the door behind her and once again, through our laughter, we could hear her calling as she stomped downstairs into the distance:

"Mam! You'll never guess what those three are…"

We wiped our eyes and sighed.

"Oh, I love your Jilly, Will. She's *such* a target. It never fails, does it?"

Then we got down to some serious business.

***

For many good reasons we decided against telling our parents the *exact* nature of our project – something I'm sure anyone with an expensive White Pearl bathroom suite and an obvious drinks cabinet in the living room would understand. I mean, let's face it, mothers just get in a state if you walk into some houses with your shoes on, let alone drag a stinky old guy in after you who hasn't had a bath since 1966. Mothers don't always recognize *Community Spirit* when they see it, but they always recognize alchoholic spirits, especially when you fall over the coffee table and pretend you've only been in the library doing homework. Ahem. Not that that has ever happened to me, of course.

No, we just told our parents we were helping the homeless and they were most impressed, apart from Gaz's mam who thought he was taking the mick because Gaz's dad probably WAS homeless. Well, they haven't seen him in years, not since he was run out of town for trying to jump across the river in the rush hour: in the Lord Mayor's Rolls-Royce. He didn't make it – well, the car didn't – and the traffic was held up for hours whilst the police tried to get him off the only bridge in and out of the town, but that's another story.

As usual we ended up deciding on my house for all the necessary arrangements. This is where we would bring Jimmy, once we had caught him, to clean him up and get him started on our *Improvement Programme* as we liked to call it. This was because my house was the one which was mostly empty while everyone was at work. You see, the school had given us a couple of hours each week during Citizenship lesson time to go out and about doing, well, whatever. This is when I realized that us three were *actually beginning to grow up a bit.* In the past, given some time out of our school day like this, we would have nicked off down into the park, or gone for a game of snooker in Rob's garage or something. But no, here we were, taking everything seriously.

We looked at the pile of clothes on the kitchen table in front of us that we had assigned to Jimmy.

"I think the shiny purple bomber jacket is a no-no," sighed Rob, casting it to one side and staring accusingly at Gaz, who tutted loudly and shrugged his shoulders. "Let's see what we've got for him and what we still need."

We had spent Saturday morning scouring every second-hand clothes shop in the area, but not before deciding that we would go in in disguise. Well, I mean, it's just not *cool,* is it? Going into Oxfam and Scope with all the grannies? Someone might see us and think WE were the charity cases. I mean, they're hardly Next or Emporio Armani, are they?

Rob had worn a hat pulled low, I put my hood up and Gaz wore Nigel's wig as we skulked into the first shop, but the old dear behind the counter threw us out and threatened to call the police: she thought we were going to rob the place. Like you would. Honestly! We managed to convince her that we really needed some clothes and had a bit rake about but then it all got quite silly and we nearly got thrown out again.

I picked up an old fur stole and called to Gaz, "Oy, Gaz, you know that ginger tom of yours who went missing last year? Well, he's here."

Then Rob came out of the changing room wearing a flowery dress three sizes too big and a pair of wellies, so we all had a good laugh at that, then Gaz began to check out the old bras and undies, which is when the manager was called.

"Right, you three, out you go."

She was a bit of a battle axe and we decided not to push our luck with her, so we explained a little bit about trying to help an elderly relative who had fallen on hard times. We didn't tell her the whole truth because we didn't want to spoil our final day of triumph when the story hit the local newspaper. Turns out she was alright really, and she got a few bits and pieces together for us.

"What size is this old chap then?" she asked. We looked blankly at each other, then at her.

"Well, he's not as big as you, any road," Gaz pointed out, a bit insensitively I thought. Her face was a picture.

As one eyebrow went up, I jumped in with, "No, he's not as healthy and attractive as this lady, Gaz. He's had a hard time of late," I told her, digging Gaz in the ribs.

"Ah, been poorly, has he?" she asked. I think we three had a vision then of the last time we had seen Jimmy, in the town centre, sitting in the middle of a roundabout, blind drunk, singing and trying to eat the daffodils.

"Oh, yes, he's often sick," Rob told her, smiling in my direction. Gaz sniggered. The manager seemed wary of Gaz, unsurprisingly. Most people who didn't know him were. Anyway, we ended up with some string vests, some Y-fronts which none of us three would handle – she had to put them in the bag for us – a warm jumper, some old, brown cord trousers and a belt.

"You can have that lot for ten pounds then," she told us with a smile. Ten quid? That would wipe us clean out. I looked at the other two. Rob just shrugged and Gaz was away down the back of the shop. Probably heading back to the underwear section again. Rob handed over our hard-earned cash and we called to Gaz to hurry up and join us at the till, then we got out of the smelly place quickly.

Outside, I was fairly shocked.

"Ten quid! And she thought she was doing us a favour!" I exclaimed.

"It IS a charity shop, mate. What did you expect?" Rob told me, looking quizzically at Gaz who was hanging back a bit and smiling to himself. Or it might have been just wind.

"Come on, Gaz. What is it?" Rob asked him patiently.

Gaz caught us up round the corner and pulled the shiny purple bomber jacket out from under his jacket with a triumphant flourish.

"Ta Da!" he sang. "That'll teach her to try to rip us off!"

Which is how we ended up with some clothes for Jimmy but no coat, hat, or shoes. Well, it was a start.

Chapter 7

We had absolutely no idea quite how we should first approach Jimmy and what to say to him so that he would listen and take us seriously. Rumour had it that as well as being a stinky, cantankerous old grouch, he was stone deaf as well.

"We'll have to time it when he's sober," Rob began.

We were all in my kitchen making something to eat and trying to stop Gaz from making a mess. I don't think they keep any food in his house, well, other than cat food. His mam has about 14 of them you see.

"Is he ever sober?" I asked, genuinely, watching Gaz eating cornflakes straight out of the box. He'd already had a cold sausage, a marmite and banana sandwich, and a raw egg in milk. Yuk. He said it was to build muscle. As he's built like an anorexic greyhound, *obviously* he hadn't had any of this before. He just makes things up as he goes along does Gaz.

"Why don't we take one of the dummies out tonight, for a laugh, and just give this Jimmy Jesus thing a break?" Gaz mumbled through a chocolate biscuit. "I mean, this thing is doing my head in. It's all we've thought about in days. Don't forget our three new friends. We haven't even had Nigel out yet."

Rob and I looked at Gaz. He had a point actually.

"Yeah, you're right, mate. It is taking over our lives a bit. We need some fun and to put some space between us and the Jimmy thing."

"Yep," I agreed. "It's Saturday night after all, and what do we normally do on a Saturday night? Go and annoy the hell out of Mad Mick!"

The lads seemed happy with that. Nothing new there then, but how to have some fun with Nigel too?

"We'd better get our thinking caps on, lads," I told them.

"We'd better get my thinking cap BACK!" Gaz announced with a smile. "And guess who has it? None other than that lumpy-bumpy Big Bird, Bernice."

We grinned at each other in silent agreement, Gaz in the process of dunking a doughnut into his glass of Irn Bru, whilst I froze in the process of eating all the little coloured sweets from the top of the fairy cakes Jilly had made that morning.

I rubbed my hands together in delight.

"Ho ho, this is gonna be a good night," I told my friends. "I can feel it in my water."

***

We decided to try some of Jimmy's new clothes on Nigel but of course we apologized profusely to him first that they were *not* going to be the height of fashion he would have been so used to wearing whilst he was the star of Dooley's "Winter Wonderland" window display. We took him into my mam and dad's room and propped him up facing the full-length mirror inside their wardrobe so Nigel could get a good look at himself. We were all quite quiet as we gazed at his reflection and looked from Nigel to each other.

"What now?" I asked.

Gaz watched Nigel as if he were sizing up a prize racehorse, while Rob walked close to the mirror to inspect him in detail then backed away and sat on Mam's bed.

"He doesn't look very happy, does he?" Rob asked.

I knew what he meant but I couldn't quite put my finger on it, so I sat on the bed beside him to get a similar view of our mate Nige.

"Prop him up, Gaz, and come and see what you think."

Gaz did as he was told, and he too joined us on my parents' big, white counterpane. The three of us sat there and stared at the dummy leaning forlornly against the wardrobe.

"Well, he's not as pretty as Flora..." Gaz began.

I hit him with a pillow.

"To me, he doesn't seem very, well, *clean*," Rob stated. "And I think he knows that. Remember, he's used to being all shiny and new, lit by the best lighting, wearing make-up and the best clothing, and hanging out with some top totty."

"Give over, man; you make him sound like George Clooney for God's sake!" I retorted.

We continued to stare at Nigel, who stared back at us, pleadingly.

"I know!" Gaz declared, getting off the bed and raking around on my mam's dressing table.

"Oy! What are you doing, Gaz?" I demanded. He turned to wink at me and Rob.

"It's ok, I know just what he needs," and he picked something off the dressing table and proceeded to remove the top half of Nigel's clothes. Rob and I groaned.

"No, Gaz, mate, I don't think roll-on deodorant is going to do the trick," Rob told him while I hung my head and giggled in quiet disbelief.

"Sure?" he asked and didn't understand why we threw another pillow at him.

"Idiot," Rob laughed back.

"Well then, can we bath him?" Gaz asked.

Rob and I thought seriously about this one for a second or two.

"No, I don't think it's a bath we need, you know. I think he looks somehow *older* than Keith and Flora," I told them.

Gaz sighed dramatically.

"Derr, that's cos he's BALD, you dummy," he explained to Rob and me patiently.

Rob thought that was great. He got off the bed and stood closer to Nigel.

"You could be right, you know, Gaz. Maybe it's the second-hand clothes, or perhaps it's the fact that his eyes are quite pale, but he DOES look older than the other two." He turned to us two, excitedly.

"Let's give him some wrinkles!"

"What, by staying out all night, getting kicked out of school, becoming drug addicts and getting a 14-year-old pregnant?" I laughed as Gaz nodded enthusiastically.

"Ha ha," Rob said sarcastically. "Has your mam got any make-up in here?"

"It's in the top left-hand drawer," Gaz told us.

Rob and I looked at each other questioningly then stared at him suspiciously.

"What?" he asked, trying to look innocent.

Five minutes later we were all four of us squeezed into the bathroom with a collection of cotton wool, eye-liner pencils, an ash tray with a couple of dog ends in and some glue. We sat Nigel down on the toilet so that he was easier to handle.

Rob had decided to give him the odd wrinkle or two and I wanted to give him some grey hair which would stick out from under his cap, when we got round to getting him one. Gaz kept trying to get Nigel to hold one of the cigarette ends, but Rob and I told him off for that. He was quite hurt.

"Oh, go on," he begged. "Loads of old guys have fag ends hanging out of their mouths. And anyway, if we burnt his fingertips, he would look realistic."

"Nigel is not a smoker," I told him firmly. "We'll have enough of a problem with Jimmy and the fags when we finally get *him* in here."

At that point we all went a bit quiet as we pondered the task of doing all this with a REAL old bloke. I shuddered, but tried to hide it from the lads.

"So, what's the ash tray for then?" Gaz asked sullenly.

"Aha, all will be revealed in a minute," I told him, rolling and stretching some of the cotton wool and trying it around the back and sides of Nigel's head for size.

"Are we not giving him a full head of hair then?" Rob asked, as I carefully dipped and rolled the wool in the old ash at the bottom of the ashtray. I just smiled, painted a bit of glue above his ears and round the back of his head then stuck on his now distinguished-looking grey hair.

"Hey!" Rob laughed, "he looks like Jean-Luc Picard now!"

Even Gaz could see the resemblance.

"Ahead warp factor five," he laughed as I started singing the Star Trek theme tune. We had just added some fine lines to his forehead and side of his nose, and stopped Gaz from giving him bright red lipstick, when we heard Jilly and the boyfriend arriving at the front door.

"Oh no. She'll have a fit if she sees Mam's bedroom!" I hissed at the lads. "You two get into my room, quickly, while I put some of this stuff away."

We legged it, Rob and Gaz tiptoeing down the hall, giggling, whilst I flew into our parents' room and started tidying the bed and stuffing all the make-up back into the drawers. I got out onto the landing in just enough time to see Jilly starting up the stairs. Steve was lounging about at the bottom: he had one foot on the bottom step to follow her before he looked up and saw me, at which point he thought better about it and stood back down again. I smiled down at him from over the banister and winked at him.

"All right, Steve?" I asked with a smug smile.

He pulled a face and answered, "All right, Will."

Jilly was making her way up and when she saw me, she started on me straight away.

"I hope you haven't been in my room, you little troll."

She edged past me, watching me carefully as if I would pounce on her at any minute.

"As if I would," I told her with a simple grin.

She walked towards her room, still watching me like a hawk, when suddenly the door to her bedroom flew open and Gaz leapt out at her, hair all over the place, hands clawing the air in front of her face, wailing like a demon.

"But *I* would!" he cackled, grabbing her round the throat.

Rob suddenly launched himself out of my room to "pull Gaz off your sister" he said later, and Steve leapt up the stairs like Sir Galahad to rescue his beloved. He laughed at her shocked expression.

"You bloody idiot, Will!" she screamed at me. "Can't you and your friends find something normal to do on a Saturday afternoon? Like, go and play with the traffic or something?"

Actually, she did look a bit spooked, so I sent the lads down to tidy up the kitchen and Steve went to supervise them. Well, guard the fridge door.

Jilly stormed into her bedroom and started opening cupboards and looking under the bed to make sure there was no-one else lurking in there. I followed her in, smoothing down her bed and straightening her Jordan Henderson poster in an attempt to get back in her favour. She was still steaming, I could tell.

"Oh, come on, Jill. Calm down now. It's not as if you were hurt or anything was damaged, is it? You know Gaz only did it because he's so much in love with you."

That stopped her in her tracks. She watched me from the mirror where she was straightening her hair.

"Honestly?" she asked. "Is he really?"

"Well, you know what his family is like? You're the nearest thing to a goddess as far as his family goes. I mean, his sister looks like Olive Oyl."

She had been calming down but then realized we had our wires crossed.

"Urgh! You mean the UGLY one? Not Rob?" And as I was puzzling this one out, she pushed past me and into the bathroom.

I called after her. "Hey, Jilly, don't tell me you fancy R..." but her screams told me she had found Nigel, sitting on the toilet where we had left him. I grabbed the lads and we bolted, down the stairs, out through the kitchen door and away over next door's garden until the coast was clear. We hid behind some wheelie bins in the back lane and laughed like drains.

A bit later, when we thought it was safe and atrocities with the enemy had eased off for the night, we rescued Nigel from the wheelie bin where "someone" had dumped him. Apart from some broken eggshell attached to his left ear, and a soggy mushroom giving him what looked like a realistic black eye, only his pride seemed hurt. His new old-man hair was surprisingly still in place and in one hand he had managed to pick up a fag end, so all in all our Nige was taking on a personality of his own. Gaz was particularly impressed.

"He even smells like a real grandad now," he smiled, tucking Nigel's shirt back into his trousers.

"Really?" asked Rob. "My grandad smells of Old Spice with a hint of kipper. It's alright actually."

"Oh, you know what?" I began. "I really like it when my grandad gives me a dead arm and a bear hug after he's been in the club on a Sunday lunchtime. He says it's the closest I'll get in years to the smell of Brown Ale. Little does he know, eh?"

We all laughed, knowingly, then silently tried to imagine sinking a pint of the stuff. Oh, the joys we had ahead of us!

We stood Nigel in our old coalhouse and promised him faithfully we'd take him out on the town with us later, when we'd all had some tea. We arranged for the lads to come back to my house at about half seven, then all four of us would go out and have some fun. In the half light of the coal house, I'd swear that Nigel gave me a smile and a thumbs up: I mean, the poor old bloke must have been watching Keith and Flora going out and about and wondering when his time would come. Not much longer now, Nige.

"Right, then, see you later. I'm off home. I'm starving," Gaz said, sloping off into the evening, hands tucked in his pockets.

"Unbelievable," I said to Robbo. "He's only eaten most of the contents of our fridge, and half the cereal in the cupboards."

"And three quarters of those little cakes your Jilly made this morning," Rob told me with a grin.

"Oh, no, that was m…" I began but then the light inside my head went on as I imagined Jilly's reaction to the devastation in the kitchen. "Yeah, you're right," I said, smiling. "Them and all."

We gave each other a fist bump and a high five and started on our way to our respective homes in opposite directions. I was smiling to myself, wanting to get into the shed to bring Ross up to date on recent developments.

I still missed our Ross. My beloved big brother, my hero. I hadn't spoken to him for a while and felt the need to tell him all about Jimmy Jesus and our plans to rescue the old guy. A couple of years after losing him, I felt like I was getting used to the empty feel our house took on sometimes, especially when Jilly was at work and Mam and Dad were out. That's when me and Ross would spend some quality time together. We would just be on the Xbox, slaying zombies, or he'd be telling me about some weirdo in Uni who still thought the earth was flat. Ross could make me howl with laughter, like when he could do all the different accents and voices of his lecturers, or the Belfast Caretaker who was scared of mops. My heart shifted inside me for a second as I thought about him. God, I missed him sometimes…

I was ambling along, smiling softly, when I bumped into the tall, sedate figure of Fr O'Rafferty, just coming out of the gates of St Peter's church. He stopped when he saw me, thrust his hands into his pockets, and a broad grin spread across his handsome dark features. He was ok, this guy.

"Will!" he greeted me amiably, folding his arms and standing steady, as if for a chat. I swallowed hard; a lump had formed in my throat and the smile had slipped from my face. I could feel myself becoming flustered. Was it all priests, or just this one that had this effect on me? I looked up at all six feet four of him. He knew.

"How are you doing, Will?" he asked me, kindly. "Been ages since I saw you. Is your mam ok?"

As I looked up at him, memories flooded my mind, bubbling up inside my head, threatening to drown me. Not good memories either. Flowers, a lone bell tolling sadly, tears, rain, crowds of people, long black cars. I felt the blackness rising up inside me.

"I'm fine, Father Jim," I told him. Should you lie to a priest? Can I still go to Heaven? Was I *ever* going there anyway?

Fr Jim looked at me with his deep brown eyes as if seeing straight into my soul. He shrugged, but told me warmly, "Will, you know where I am if you or your family ever need me. It's never too late, you know."

I nodded, tried to smile at him, and started to shuffle on, my heart heavy inside my ribs. Memories were coursing through my head and my heart like a sugar rush; I nearly said *drugs* there… What the…? I'd only gone a couple of steps when the priest called after me.

"Remember – I could always use a hand in Peter's Place. They'd love you and your mates in there, Will."

I turned back to face him. "Really, Father Jim? And lose all my street cred?"

The priest gave me a salute. I grinned back at him.

"Aye, maybe one day. To say thanks," I told him, and headed for home, my heart feeling a little heavier than before.

Chapter 8

Rob had this idea that now that Nigel was a gentleman of advanced years, it would be unseemly to try to get him off with "a young bit of fluff" as he so delicately put it.

"Here, why should he get all the luck? If anyone's going on the pull, it should be one of us," I said, staring from one to the other. "It is Saturday night, after all."

We stood in silence for a second or two and considered this valid point, each of us eyeing up the opposition, so to speak. Rob was the first to give his considered opinion.

"Actually, you've got a point there, mate," he said. "Which one of us three is at the top of his game and really deserves to get the girl?"

Gaz picked up the challenge. "Yeah, which one of us is a cool guy who no woman can ever resist?"

I swear he even smoothed an eyebrow here and stood a little out of his slouch.

"Which one of us simply *oozes* sex appeal and has the best chat up lines in the business?" I asked, shrugging nonchalantly.

After a moment spent scanning our fairly desperate faces we decided, resignedly, in unison, "Nigel."

He was leaning against the park railings at that point and began to slide to the ground as none of us were hanging on to him.

"Here, don't look so thrilled, me old mate," Rob told him, grabbing him by his lapels and hauling him to his feet.

"At least one of us might be on a promise!"

There followed an in-depth discussion about which delightful destinations in our bustling and buzzing town we would take Nige to; well, by in-depth I mean me suggesting somewhere and the other two grimacing and going:

"Nah!"

"No chance!"

"You thick or something?"

and "Get a life".

Gaz was barred from McDonald's – don't ask – the Hotspot youth club was shut on a Saturday and we'd managed to frighten away all those lovely year ten girls who used to hang around our park. I think it was Gaz's David Beckham impersonation that did it. The girls just think he's a weirdo freak now. Gaz, that is, not Beckham.

"There's a disco on at that church centre. We could go there for a change," Rob suggested.

"Nah, it's grab a granny night on Saturdays," Gaz said.

"Perfect!" I announced.

"You what? You want to try to pull some old bird of about 40?"

"D'uh, not for me, dipstick, for Nige," I told them, straightening his jacket. Then the penny dropped, and they smiled.

"Come on, son, your luck just changed," Rob told the dummy as he and I picked him up between us. "You're going to have a good night after all."

The vicar on the door took one look at us four and told us to bugger off.

"Very Christian, I must say," retorted Rob.

We hung around outside for a while, hoping to catch the eye of one or two old girls, coming along in their finery for a night of fancy footwork and the odd Babycham or two. Gaz nipped around the back and came back with a half empty bottle of lager, one of those little ones you get from a booze cruise.

"Gaz, man, what good is one little bottle of lager between four of us?" asked Rob.

"Just watch," he said. He stood Nigel against the low wall at the front of the church hall and placed the bottle in one of the dummy's hands. Then he bent down and picked up a cigarette butt which he put into Nigel's other hand.

"Right, lads, get behind the wall and shut up."

We did as we were told and got behind the wall. I could see a plan starting to take shape. We crouched there, peeping out occasionally, waiting for more guests to arrive at the entrance. It was fairly dark by now and Nige cut quite a dashing figure in the half light of the church doorway, if I say so myself. Rob had been on lookout and popped back down behind the wall.

"Two of them, incoming. They look as if they've already been at the cooking sherry as well."

We waited until the two women stopped at the start of the church path. One of them was raking inside a cavernous handbag whilst the other waited for her friend.

"Oh, hurry up, Doreen," she said, "you can look properly inside."

Doreen was not going to hurry up. She continued searching her handbag. "Look, if that bloke Arthur is in again tonight, I want my best lippy on. He might ask me out this week. My star signs say my luck has turned."

"Star signs? My arse!" retorted her friend.

At that point I let out a low wolf whistle from behind the wall. We three started to giggle.

Rob decided to use his best old gadgey voice. He sounded like Clint Eastwood after a week's holiday in South Shields.

"Hello Doreen. Is that you, my lovely lass? I thought you weren't coming tonight. I've been freezing my walnuts off out here."

Peeping my head over the wall I could see Doreen and her mate freeze and look towards Nigel. By now Gaz was on the ground trying to eat grass to stop himself from laughing out loud. I kicked him to stop him from giving away our position. Well, I often have to kick Gaz. I think he likes it really.

"Eeh, Arthur, is that you?" Doreen asked. "You look a bit pale. You haven't had that swine flu, have you?"

Her voice was full of anxious concern. I watched as both women started preening themselves in preparation of meeting up with the object of their desires again.

"No, no, girls. I've just been pining for the company of a couple of real beauties. And here they are. Come and have a dance with me. Now, which one's going to go first?"

I was full of admiration for my mate Rob by then. Was there anything this lad wasn't good at?

As we heard two sets of footsteps start forward, we three couldn't resist popping up from behind the wall to watch. I tell you, these two best friends nearly killed each other as they elbowed and nudged each other out of the way to get to "Arthur" first. We watched in round-eyed glee as first Doreen, then her friend, stopped dead in their tracks and stared at Nigel.

"What on earth…" began Doreen.

"Well, I never!" exclaimed her friend, picking the lager bottle from Nigel's hand and sniffing it, as if that may be a clue as to who or what this guy was doing there. One of them then grabbed Nigel by the neck and started shaking him, in surprised – and disappointed – disgust, as he was not the man of their dreams, waiting in the moonlight for them, after all. We three jumped over the wall, falling about with laughter to rescue our lothario.

Rob couldn't resist telling the ladies in his Clint Eastwood voice, "Now, now, girls, don't get rough. Form an orderly queue and we'll talk about which one of you has me first."

I thought we were going to get lynched, I tell you. We bundled Nigel out of harm's way and ran off with him into the night, to howls of angry abuse and a well-aimed bottle of lager, which went spinning past my left ear. As we came to rest behind an old gravestone in the cemetery, Rob declared breathlessly, "I told you we'd have a laugh tonight, lads."

***

Later, sitting on a wall near the chip shop, sharing a couple of bags between the four of us, the conversation turned to Jimmy and what on earth we were going to do with him. It could have been that Nigel was actually much heavier to carry than Keith and Flora, or that he was just naturally a clumsy old goat, but we had struggled to get him away from the church hall in one piece. We sat him in the middle of us to stop him from falling over and whenever anyone local walked past, we raised Nigel's hand in casual salute. Well, old blokes generally have good manners, don't they? They were brought up properly, like, we decided. We weren't taking the p...er, mickey, at all. We were just nice lads out to have a laugh. And Nigel was enjoying himself, after all the fun outside the church: a bit tired, but still happy to be sitting there in such stimulating and cheerful good company. I think after battling with a pretendy old bloke, the enormity of what we had said we would do with a real life stinky old guy like Jimmy was settling in. None of us had the bottle to actually come out and say that Rob's idea of adopting a tramp and taming him was really mad. Brilliant – but mad. And I had the sneaking suspicion that our teacher was just taking the mick and waiting for us to come a cropper. Let's face it, we normally did, and not just in his lessons either. We were renowned for it. Rob sensed my hesitation.

"Lads, have I ever let you down before? You know we can do this. Once we find out where Jimmy is hiding out, it'll be a doddle. Which old fella in his right mind wouldn't want a warm bed, a hot bath and food whenever he needs it?"

"Yeah, but that's just it," I told him. "Jimmy hasn't been in his right mind for years. We don't know *what* he thinks, if he *can* still think after years of boozing himself senseless on the streets."

We sat there, chewing our chips reflectively.

Once in a while, when a couple of old blokes wandered past us on their way from the pub, one or two of them grunted "All right, Tommy?" at us in response to Nigel's raised arm. After the third time, Robbo grunted back at them, a sort of "Hurnff," which obviously meant something in old-bloke-speak because one of them chuckled and replied with a "grnff" before ambling off, head down. We thought this was great and spent a happy half hour "Grnff-ing" at anyone over the age of 60 and raising Nigel's arm at them. We thought it was probably some code they'd all worked on in the war and only used on a Saturday night, when warm memories or Brown Ale brought it all flooding back. I said that they probably kept it a secret, so as to confuse their enemies even further. That was us: teenage enemies. Mind you, not one of those old blokes thought it was strange that "Tommy" was sitting on a wall, eating chips out of a bag with three teenaged hoodies.

"They must think he's safe with us," I commented.

"Says a lot about us three, that does," Rob replied, "that an old guy like Nigel is safe with us. I mean, aren't we supposed to be threatening and dangerous? Keeping people inside their homes with our terror tactics on a Saturday night?" He seemed a bit cheesed off, actually.

"Maybe they think we've kidnapped him," Gaz said, screwing his chip paper up and throwing it at a rubbish bin on a bus stop. It missed, of course, and rolled onto the road before blowing across clear to the other side. We cheered and it made us all feel a bit better then, harder, and more aggressive, until Rob told him, "Gaz, you plonker. Don't show us all up. Pick up your rubbish and put it in the bin!"

As Gaz got up and apologetically strolled over to cross the road, I shook my head.

"Aye, real hard cases we are, aren't we, lads? Public enemy number one."

Gaz dodged the traffic nimbly and started to make his way back to us, but he stopped and stared hard at something back over the road, in the small park. "Lads!" he hissed, beckoning us forward. "Quick, come here."

Leaving Nige on the wall, we ambled over to see what had caught his attention. It was a bit gloomy by then so we couldn't make out what he was looking at.

"Is it that Lamborghini again?" I asked, straining into the road.

"No, I bet it's Fiona and the girls again," smiled Robbo, jumping up and down to get a better view.

Neither of us could see anything out of the ordinary though. A woman was walking her dog on the grass over the road, and a clapped-out old Volvo spluttered by, but nothing remarkable enough to cause the tension in Gaz's voice.

"Look – through the trees," he said, pointing.

A figure was shambling about, with Gaz's chip paper in his hand, head down, muttering to himself. We watched as he opened the chip paper up, sniffed it, then threw it to the ground again in disgust.

"Jimmy!" we exclaimed quietly, together.

"Quick, think of something before he gets away," hissed Rob.

"I'll run over and jump on him while you two…" began Gaz, but I held him back.

"Hang on," I started, "you can't just go around jumping on old guys in the middle of town. We'll get arrested."

"And he might have a heart attack. Or lamp you one," Rob said, looking doubtful. "Plus, I'm not hanging onto him in that state. He's filthy!" He shuddered.

"Let's just follow him and see where he's headed. That way we will get an idea about where he's bedding down these days."

We were just about to start over the road after Jimmy when we heard an elderly voice behind us say, "You spent all those winnings already, Tommy? Good on yer mate." An old bloke was just coming out of the chip shop and was talking to the dummy. Nigel was gazing our way and not looking at the old fella but that didn't seem to bother either of them.

"Nigel," I reminded the lads, as we turned back to get him. After all, four heads are better than three in a crisis, and I had a feeling that this would turn into one.

Keeping a safe distance, we followed Jimmy through the park, across an industrial estate and towards the docks. Every now and then the tramp stopped to rake through a dustbin or a bag of rubbish at the roadside. He growled at an old dog and aimed a kick at it just to be on the safe side as he weaved his way to wherever he was headed. Once he stopped at a grotty corner off-licence and started singing through the front door, which opened just enough for a large empty box to be hurled at him. Jimmy lurched backwards and shook an angry fist at the shop before shuffling off. He was approaching the train yard and stopped, staring in as if wondering whether it was safe to proceed. We hid behind a parked car, watching as he rocked gently on his feet. There would be plenty of sheds in the train yard where he could bed down for the night, but we knew Mad Mick the security guard of old: no-one would get within 50 feet of his shed before old radar lugs was up and at them. We knew that Mick could hear a fly fart at 50 metres. Jimmy obviously decided it was worth the risk. Without a backwards glance he tottered in through the entrance of the yard.

"Yahey!" Robbo shouted in a stage whisper. "It is Saturday night after all, lads. Come on. We don't want to disappoint Mad Mick now, do we?"

I groaned, rubbing my shoulder after the effort of lugging Nigel all that way. He was starting to look quite animated now – all the action and excitement of a night on the town with the lads was getting to him.

He certainly had some colour in his cheeks. So did me and Gaz who had to carry him. We were worn out.

"Right," I began. "If we're going in there, after Jimmy…"

"And Mick," sniggered Gaz.

"I vote we leave Nigel here for a bit. My arms are aching."

"Yeah. We need more hands to catch Jimmy anyway," Gaz told us, looking worryingly pleased about the whole thing. So, with apologies, we lay Nigel down behind a garden wall, telling him he would be quite safe and that we'd be back as soon as we'd rounded up old Jimmy. My mouth felt quite dry at the thought of it, but I didn't let the lads know that. I mean, all for one and one for all, eh? Together we started towards the entrance to the rail yard.

Chapter 9

We were just edging forward gingerly when we heard the unmistakable sound of a warthog eating a mattress – well, Mick's voice. It was a sound to strike fear into the heart of any sane men, and we were certainly not sane men. Well, sane OR men.

We ducked down out of sight behind a van. Mick had obviously caught Jimmy trying to sneak into the yard and was escorting him back out again. And by that, I mean he was doing just that – escorting him. We watched in disbelief as Mick gently held Jimmy's greasy elbow and led him to the front gate. There was a look of patience on the guard's face, and none of his usual surliness. We couldn't get our heads around this and shrugged our shoulders at each other.

"Eh? What the...?" mouthed Rob to me. I just frowned back. As we watched, Mick put his hand into the pocket of his donkey jacket and placed something in Jimmy's grubby mitt before carefully guiding him on down the street.

"There you are, mate. Get yourself a nice hot cuppa. Ta-ra, old fella. See you next time."

Mick stood and watched as Jimmy ambled off on his way, chuntering on to himself cheerfully, bouncing off the odd wall. Mick turned after a second or two and went back into the bowels of Hell – well, into the train yard, I mean.

Rob was the first to comment on what we had just witnessed.

"Well, flying flatfish! What do you make of that?"

"I thought the old guy was going to get a right pasting there," I said.

"You don't think Mick really does have a heart, do you?" asked Gaz. We pondered that for a second and were just about to agree he could be right, before Gaz added, "I mean, he does go out with Big Bird, you know."

Well, that killed it for me. "The only thing Mad Mick has a heart for is frightening the bejaysus out of us three on a Saturday night," I told them.

"Yeah, and for downing pints of brown ale in the club and taking on a brace of bouncers in town for a laugh," Rob replied.

"Is that really what you call a couple of bouncers then?" asked Gaz. "A brace?"

"You can call them anything you like, if you can run a two-minute mile," I told them, laughing and remembering some fun we had had at their expense last summer. We were nearly run out of town, but that's another story.

In the next street we waited behind and watched as Jimmy bent down shakily to pick a fag end off the ground. He hiccupped and held it up to the streetlight as if checking to see if it was useable.

"Oh no, he's not going to really put that in his mouth, is he?" wailed Rob.

"I think a fag end is the least worrying thing Jimmy's had in his mouth. And just think, it's going to be our job to tell him what he can and can't eat if we get to look after him," I reminded the lads.

"Urgh. He's not going to *eat* that, is he?" asked Gaz, incredulously.

We were giggling about Gaz being as thick as ever when three men came round the bend and stopped over the road from Jimmy. For some reason I held the lads back, not wanting the men to see that we were following Jimmy, but also because some deep instinct told me to keep away from something unpleasant which may have been about to unfold.

"Hang on a second, lads," I told them, holding each back by an arm.

Rob looked at me in concern. He knows me too well, that lad. Before either of us could say anything, one of the men started pointing at Jimmy and laughing, but not in a happy, look-at-that-daft-old-sod sort of way. There was a cold nastiness to his laughter which made my mouth go dry and my knees wobble. The second, larger of the men, folded his arms and rocked on his feet a little as he watched the tramp trying to put the fag end into his mouth. He tapped his two friends on the arms, pointed towards Jimmy and said fairly loudly, "Oy, you, you smelly owld git. You want something in yer mouth then?"

His friends cackled in delight. They seemed to be enjoying themselves and obviously thought their mate was hysterical. We watched in safety behind an overgrown bush as together they crossed the road to our side, right towards Jimmy.

"I don't like the look of this," began Rob, quietly. "We should do something."

"Like what?" I asked. "There's three of them and they're at least 30 years old. What good are us three puny little whippets going to be?"

Jimmy had started grunting at them, obviously thinking that here were three blokes who might also give him the price of a pint, just like the last kind fella had. He gave them a gummy grin and staggered towards them, hands held out, fag in mouth. One of the men snatched the cigarette end out of Jimmy's mouth and threw it to the ground. The other two sniggered sarcastically.

"You don't want to be putting that in your mouth, granddad," he said, taking a packet of cigarettes out of his pocket and waving them in front of Jimmy's face. I heard Rob exhale in relief then and realized that I too had been holding my breath.

"Phew," whispered Gaz, "I thought things were going to get ugly there."

I didn't *think*; I knew they were.

"Here, you want something in your mouth?" asked the bloke holding the cigarettes. He turned and nodded to the smaller of his two friends then who immediately stepped forward and punched Jimmy hard in the mouth. In shock we looked on as the tramp staggered backwards and fell to the ground, making a surprised grunting noise. Rob closed his eyes and turned away. I heard Gaz beside me make a sort of whimpering sound as he held on tight to my sleeve. I wanted to run straight out, but I was terrified. My face was screwed up in torment and my breath was ragged. What could we do?

The other man, the one who up until then hadn't done much other than grin inanely, strolled forward casually and kicked the tramp hard in the stomach, as he lay on the ground holding his hands to his mouth. Whack!

As I doubled up in his agony, I heard the air rush painfully out of Jimmy, and he started gasping for breath. This seemed to please the three thugs enormously. They laughed and high-fived each other in delight. Jimmy lay on the ground, groaning and rocking. I felt tears welling up in my eyes and wanted to scream in frustration at seeing this innocent old bloke being treated like this. I knew, however, that there was nothing we could do to help. If we were to step forward, we would get the same treatment. We couldn't help. We were helplessly impotent. They were men and would not take us seriously.

The first bloke started ramming cigarettes into Jimmy's battered, bleeding old mouth. He started choking and gagging on them, waving his arms around pathetically in an attempt to ward off his attackers. Beside me, Rob whimpered, feeling Jimmy's pain. The thug simply laughed louder, telling Jimmy, "There you are, you old bastard. You wanted a fag? Now you've got one!"

Gaz had dropped down to the ground behind the bush. He was weeping in despair. I stood there, just rooted to the spot in horror. I thought they were about to kill old Jimmy. I prayed silently and fervently for help to arrive from somewhere. All three of the men now stood over Jimmy. One of them got a lighter out and flicked it on with the flame turned up high. It flared threateningly in the gloom, illuminating the hellish scene in front of us. I gasped in horror at what might happen to the old guy next. I shut my eyes tighter. I'm ashamed to say I then too turned away. I felt sick and helpless.

Suddenly Rob ran forward. He threw off our attempts to hold him back and ran into the circle of light two streetlamps down from the attackers. Gaz and I groaned in disbelief.

"Yes, officer, they're right here now," he announced into his mobile. I somehow found the presence of mind to think, what mobile? Rob was cupping his hand to his right ear and was waving to someone as if they were right around the corner. "They're trying to set fire to this old guy and have beaten him up! They're right in front of me, officer, quick!"

Huh? The police were here already? That *was* quick, and very unusual as well, especially for this part of town. Gaz and I also stepped forward now that reinforcements were arriving. Gaz got out his mobile and started *filming* the three thugs. I looked at him in disbelief! We wanted to see these three get arrested, but I mean, come on. How soon were the keystone cops going to be?! I thought we were about to be minced as well, if the attackers saw what we were doing and grabbed us just for the fun of it.

Suddenly the three men stopped their attack on Jimmy and glared at Rob before looking behind him towards me and Gaz. We stood there, fists clenched and breathing hard as they suddenly gave up and sprinted off into the night. One of them looked back at us and seemed about to make a move forward but changed his mind at the last minute.

"You've seen nothing, you understand, you little bastards?!" Before he, too, legged it.

We moved towards the still groaning and bloodied Jimmy. My legs had turned to jelly, and I found it hard to walk but I wasn't going to let the lads see that.

"So where are the cops then, Rob? I didn't see you call them," I began. Rob smiled grimly and bent down to the old guy groaning on the ground.

"There are no cops. There is no mobile. I just pretended there was," he said. "Mine's still on charge in my bedroom. I came out without it." He shrugged his shoulders.

"Luckily for you they didn't know that," Gaz told him. "Otherwise, we'd all have got what they gave Jimmy here."

Together we helped Jimmy to his feet, but he swore and swung at us as if he thought we were attacking him as well. We tried to reason with him, but he pushed us roughly away and staggered off on his own, leaving us feeling sick and sad, standing there under the glaring streetlight, pathetic and miserable.

"We should stop him and get him cleaned up," I said, watching as Jimmy coughed up blood and spat it into the gutter, before lurching painfully on his way.

"No, mate, let's just go home. I've had enough for tonight," Rob stated sadly.

We looked at each other for a second, each registering our unspoken horror and impotence at what we had just witnessed. We knew without saying a word how we were all feeling, how ashamed we felt at the inhumanity we had seen. Then Gaz spoke up, angrily.

"Well, you two can bugger off home if you like, but I'm going to call an ambulance for that old guy. I don't believe you! He could be collapsed round that corner with broken ribs or having a heart attack and you two just want to give up on him and crawl back home to your mammies!"

He pushed past us and stormed off on his way. Rob and I looked at each other, feeling ashamed. We knew he was right. We had to gather up the strength and maturity from somewhere and help.

"Hang on, Gaz," Rob said sadly. "We're right behind you, old mate. Aren't we, Will?"

I caught up to the two of them and punched Gaz on his arm, cos he likes that. It's like a badge of honour to him.

"Strewth, yeah, mate. We're in this together. All for one... and..."

"And all that crap," smiled Gaz. Then he stopped dead and got out his phone again. I looked ahead at what appeared to be a bundle of old rags lying in the middle of the road, until that bundle groaned. Jimmy. He looked even more pathetic than ever. I bit my lip and tried not to cry.

"Ambulance please," requested Gaz and you know, for a minute or two, he was the calmest and most controlled young man I'd seen in a long time. I hardly recognized him.

Chapter 10

By the time the ambulance arrived, we had managed to move Jimmy to the pavement, and were gingerly attempting to sit him against a wall whilst trying to reassure the old bloke that we were not going to kill him. We talked quietly to him at first, then realized he was probably stone deaf, so Rob started yelling at him.

"Can you breathe all right, Jimmy?" at the top of his voice.

"Rob, man…" I began, looking around the street for nosey passers-by to come along and join in.

"Keep it down a bit. You don't want to burst his eardrums as well as his ribs, do you?"

We had found a wadge of loo roll in one of my pockets and held it to his battered mouth, but the old fella looked in a bad way. Jimmy was pale, and his skin looked clammy.

"He's not breathing very well, is he?" I asked.

Gaz was fishing about in his pockets. He crouched down beside Jimmy on the pavement.

"Here, mate," he said, offering something small and blue to the old guy. Jimmy looked at it and sniffed it suspiciously.

"What's that you're giving him, Gaz?" asked Rob.

"Chewy. One of those extra strong, minty ones. His mouth is a mess and it'll freshen him up a bit," Gaz replied.

Rob and I smiled at each other. Our mate was back in proper Gaz mode. For a fleeting minute I wanted to kiss him.

"That's a lovely gesture, Gaz, but I think we'll leave that to the professionals, eh? He might be, you know, nil by mouth." Gently, Rob removed the uneaten piece of chewy from Jimmy's filthy hand.

Gaz was by this time sitting with his arm around Jimmy who was trembling like a leaf, and looking old, cold and in pain. At that point, I heard the wail of the siren.

"Thank God for that," I said out loud. The responsibility was beginning to get to me, and I couldn't wait to hand the old chap over to someone – *anyone* basically – but preferably someone who knew what they were doing. I wanted to go home and have a long hot soak in the bath. I felt grubby and sour, and I had a feeling it wasn't just from being in such close contact with Jimmy Jesus.

Rob stepped into the road to flag down the ambulance and it rolled to a stop with a double "whoop", a flash of blue lights and the reassuring sound of banging doors. Two guys in green uniforms jumped out and came to crouch down beside Jimmy.

"All right then, lads?" one asked, suspiciously, I thought. "What happened here then?"

"Three blokes jumped him and attacked him," Rob told them. "We couldn't really do anything to help him."

The ambulance driver looked from Rob, to me, to Gaz, his eyes scanning the scene and missing nothing, whilst his partner tended to the battered old man.

"Oh yeah? Three of them, you say?"

I looked at Rob and shook my head. The penny had dropped for him and I could see two pink spots forming on his cheeks, a sure sign that his temper was rising, and he was going to blow, big time.

"No, no mate. You've got it all wrong," I jumped in quickly before Rob blew a gasket. "We were just following the old guy and we saw three men attack him."

You know when you say something, and before it's out you wish you could swallow your own teeth, let alone the words which have just spilled out of your own stupid mouth? Well, it was one of those times.

"You were just *following* him?" The paramedic asked, too casually for my liking. "The *three* of you?"

He had leaned Jimmy forward and was listening to his back through a stethoscope. Rob had stood up and was pulling at his hair in frustration.

"You cannot think we were responsible for this?" he stormed.

The other paramedic stood up too, facing up to the angry Rob.

"Just seems a bit odd to us, son. We see stuff like this all the time. Some people get their kicks from giving old blokes like this a good hiding."

Rob and I were speechless, until we heard a forceful voice behind us say.

"Look – he's my granddad. We were just looking out for him!"

We spun round. Gaz?

"I can show you on my mobile, if you don't believe us. Three guys ran away, towards the bridge."

The two ambulance men visibly relaxed then. They started gently ushering Jimmy towards the wagon, folded up as he was like a crumpled brown paper bag.

"Ah, that's alright then, son. Sorry. We have to check." He opened the back doors and helped Jimmy inside, where they sat him down and covered him with a bright red blanket. The interior light threw a greenish glow across Jimmy's wrinkled, pale face. Rob and I sighed in relief and gave Gaz a thumbs up for his quick thinking. I began to back away from the vehicle: I could hear that scented hot bath bubbling and running in my frazzled mind. I was just about to get hold of my mates and take them back up the road when the driver said: "You'll be wanting to travel to the hospital with him then. Up you get."

And before Rob or I could protest, in Gaz got, with a cheery little wave to us. The ambulance drove off with another "whoop", leaving me and Rob standing there, open mouthed in the road. I could feel the bubbles draining away down the plughole in my mind. I turned to look at Rob who shook his head grimly.

"Now what?" I asked him.

"To the hospital, I guess," he told me with a sigh which came up from his boots.

***

"No way, mate," I told Rob. "I'm not going in there. You can't make me."

I hate hospitals. They're worse than our Jilly's goulash, my granddad's feet, Alan Carr's gob and stinky school cabbage all rolled into one. And of course, I had been in A&E before, on that horrendous dark day not that long ago. We were standing by the entrance and even the Holby City theme tune hummed by Rob didn't make me smile.

"Look, Will, Gaz is in there somewhere, probably dropping us right in it as we speak. We've GOT to go in. This is hard for you, I know, especially after... but we really don't have a choice."

I peeped through the automatic doors as they opened to allow a woman in a wheelchair through. One side of her face was all swollen, her hair was partly shaved, and her right arm was in a sling. I shuddered, bile rising to my throat as I tried not to watch her.

"Nah – no way, man. I'm outta here."

In my mind's eye, I was getting a flashback of Ross being wheeled into this part of this very same hospital, pale-faced, lifeless. I could still hear the squeak of running shoes down the corridor and the urgent information being passed over the limp body of my big brother. It was too much to see again. I couldn't do it.

I started to walk away but Rob caught me by the elbow and spun me back towards the entrance.

"Lad, you're such a wimp," he told me. "But don't worry cos I am too; we'll just shout out to Gaz to make sure he's doing fine then we'll be out of here at warp factor five. Ok?"

Gulping in air like a goldfish, and shaking, I allowed myself to be guided inside by my mate.

I glanced sideways through the plate glass, just looking for an excuse to disappear pretty quick, when I spotted Gaz standing by the reception desk. Then I felt a bit guilty: poor Gaz, having to take all the flak just cos I had a hospital phobia. I must have looked a bit green about the gills because Rob stared hard at me; I stared back.

"What?" I demanded.

Rob began to smile. Then he started to giggle a bit, his shoulders were shaking.

"Don't you remember, Will?" he asked me.

I gave him a puzzled look.

"Yeah," I told him. "I remember all too well, Rob. That's why I can't be in here. And it really wasn't funny, trust me."

Rob looked shame-faced then. He blushed, pushing his hands through his hair.

"No, not *that* time, Will. I wouldn't do that to you, would I? I was thinking about when you were little…"

He suddenly cupped his hands in front of his nose and began making a buzzing noise. He flapped his hands out sideways and ran around in a little circle. People in the entrance looked over at his crazy little dance and smiled. I felt myself relax a little at his antics and found myself smiling back at him. It was one of Rob's favourite stories about me and my childhood. Another reason for my phobia.

I'd been like this since I was five and a bee flew up my nose. Everybody had a fit, screaming and trying to poke things up there, but I had calmed down by the time I got to the hospital. I was sitting reasonably cheerfully, in the accident department, when I thought I heard it buzzing again, so in my terror I got up and ran straight into a glass door. I knocked myself out, broke my nose and the door. Later I learned that the buzzing I'd heard was a saw in the plaster room, taking a cast off someone's broken leg. I hadn't been near the place since we lost Ross, and bees – and electric saws – still bug me big time.

Now here I was, trying to get in to rescue my mate Gaz from the jaws of death. Well, from the nurse asking him questions with a clipboard in her hand. I calmed down and tried to think of a solution. The image of Ross was fading, thankfully.

Beside me Rob was craning to have a closer look.

"Hey, she's a bit tasty, Will. I think Gaz may need our help after all."

When I looked questioningly at him, he grabbed the back of my head and forced it in the direction of the nurse Gaz was talking to. Aha! A curvy little blonde in a blue uniform.

"Do you know who that is?" I asked Rob.

"The Angel Gabriel's little sister?" he replied, eyebrows raised.

"Nearly. It's Fiona Bridges' big sister."

His eyes grew as round as gobstoppers. We grinned at each other, smoothed our hair down and marched into the Casualty department. Phobia? What hospital phobia?

Thirty minutes later and I was still inside a hospital casualty ward without fainting or throwing up. Now that is a record for me. Yeah, alright: I know I looked like a tit – wearing a face mask – but it did take my mind off the smell. The Jimmy smell, I mean, as much as the ucky hospital smell. Anyway, after grabbing a pair of surgical gloves and the mask, and giving a couple of choruses of "Beat It", I was in a much better mood than before. Some of the old dears waiting in wheelchairs gave us a round of applause when Rob picked up a mop as a microphone and Gaz did the whole crotch-grabbing Michael Jackson dance routine. Nurse Bridges – be still, my beating heart – took them off us with a stern look, but she did smile and tell the patients, "Honestly, please don't encourage them. We'll never get rid of them."

A young Irish doctor asked us to wait a bit while he examined Gaz's "granddad". We sat on three green chairs, staring dumbly at a running LED advert for waiting times, salmonella and swine flu.

"I tell you what, Gaz," I began, "that was inspired thinking on your behalf, old son. Telling them Jimmy was your granddad."

"Thanks, Will. It was, wasn't it?" He was grinning at me in a very self-satisfied sort of way. "I actually thought he looked a bit like Nigel, and you know how fond I'd become of him, so it just sort of followed on naturally," Gaz told me.

"Only don't think you can stash Jimmy behind a wall when he comes out," I told him, wondering if Nige was safe and warm. Whilst we were waiting, we had decided we would collect the dummy on the way home.

"Yeah, just as long as they don't discharge him into your care," Rob stated.

"Who? Nigel?" I asked with a frown.

"No, idiot. Jimmy." Rob watched the two of us carefully, his eyebrows raised, waiting for the penny to drop. He continued. "They won't let the old guy back out onto the streets now, will they, not now they think he has a family to look after him."

We all went quiet for a few minutes whilst we digested this unsavoury thought.

"Ah," said Gaz.

'Er...' I began.

"Exactly," stated Rob.

We sat like that a while, as patients and nurses glided past us. No-one spoke, not even when Nurse Bridges sailed past us with a cheery wave.

"Look, lads..." I started, "wasn't this exactly what we said we would do anyway? You know... the project?"

Rob shrugged. "Not really. I just came up with it to get us out of detention in Citizenship. I never thought for one minute we'd actually have to *do* anything with a stinky old homeless bloke."

Both Gaz and I turned on him, a look of shocked horror on our faces.

"You what? So why did we go to all that trouble with Nigel, raking around second-hand clothes shops and making the dummy look like an old bloke?"

Gaz joined in too, obviously struggling to get his head around Rob's about-face as well.

"You said it would be a dummy run before we actually caught Jimmy. You said we'd get an A* for our project…"

"…AND probably get our pictures in the papers as well," I reminded him.

Rob looked shame-faced about it. He sat back and stared at the ceiling, then dropped his gaze to me and Gaz.

"It was …you know…fun. A laugh. Especially messing about with the dummies. But then you two got so caught up in the whole Let's-rescue-Jimmy-Jesus-from-himself idea and I just went with it."

"Yeah," I told him. "But Jimmy isn't a dummy, is he, Rob? And that's really got you spooked, now that you're so close to actually having to put your money where your mouth is."

He was silent for a while, then suddenly stood up and looked up and down the corridor.

"Right, come on, you two."

"Where we going now?" asked Gaz.

"Out of here. Home. Anywhere. Let's just leg it. You didn't give them your real name and address, did you?"

He started to move off towards the main doors, with us two plodding behind him like sheep, when the young doctor reappeared.

"Ah, Gaz. Going for a coffee, are you? Well, I just need to ask you a few more questions about your granddad, if you don't mind."

Rob and I looked at each other and sighed. Well, that answered Rob's question anyway. Gaz shrugged a "sorry" at us and turned back to the doctor.

I tell you, I was absolutely furious with Rob. He'd got us all into this mess and here he was, trying to wriggle out of it, leaving sad, desperate old Jimmy behind in the lurch. Whilst Gaz was in the office talking to the young doctor, Rob and I glared at each other in the corridor; we were worn out and unhappy, scowling at each other in an unfamiliar way. I wondered if I'd ever really known him. Where was my mate, the superstar footballer? Where was my hero who successfully chatted up Fiona Bridges and got her into the Drama stock cupboard? Where was the brainbox who dreamed up the idea of saving a sad old bloke off the streets, making us three doofers look like caring, compassionate cool-as-ice kids?

"I don't know where to begin..." I shook my head at Rob, disbelieving.

"Will..." he began, "they'll put him in care. He won't be just chucked out. They'll find him somewhere nice, with his own room and company, and visitors and...and a telly."

"Rob, can you really see Jimmy in one of those places?" I asked. "They're awful! There's no dignity in there. And the old people sit for hours on their own, smelling of wee. Nobody gives a toss!"

"But we would," Rob answered hotly. "We'd go and visit him. Maybe take him out once in a while. Honestly, Will. It's for the best. We're not up to the responsibility of looking after him."

Just then, some way up the corridor, we heard a huge commotion. There was the sound of a kidney dish being dropped onto the tiled floor, followed by an unintelligible bellow which sounded like a bear crashing out of the undergrowth.

A red-faced nurse came stumbling backwards out of the side room, obviously very upset, and stood shaking in the corridor. Of course, when a damsel in distress calls, all arguments are forgotten, so Rob and I hurried towards her looking concerned and grown up. Sort of. At the same time, Gaz and the young Irish doctor popped their heads out of the office to see what was going on. They also joined us outside the side ward door. And what a sight met us.

The curtains around the bed had been half ripped off and were hanging drunkenly from a few of their rings. A water jug had been spilled and was dripping all over the locker top, and Jimmy was half in and half out of the bed. His greasy grey hair stood up on end, his eyes were wild, but the gown he was supposed to be wearing was on the wrong way round so the open bit was at the front. With one foot on the floor and the other on the bed all his dangly bits were on display. NOT a pretty sight.

"He's... *crawling!*" the nurse stammered, holding a swab in one hand.

"No, he's just trying to get off the bed," Rob told her, stepping forward to hold the two bits of the open gown closed. She was a brave woman I can tell you. She was short, podgy – and ginger. I don't mean that's what made her brave: her close proximity to a near naked Jimmy earned her that accolade. I stood there, blushing like an idiot, helpless in my horror. The nurse brandished the swab towards us. I leaned back away from it.

"No, I mean he's covered in lice! Look!"

We looked down at her hand with the cotton wool in it and sure enough, amongst the smudgey goo, something moved. That was it for us. We leapt back into the corridor and stood wide eyed and shaking, as Jimmy continued to climb about the bed as if he was trying to scale Everest, wailing all the time like an injured moose. The nurse flung the mess into a near bin and began beating at the front of her uniform. At that point, the Irish doctor waded in.

"Nurse Bliss!" he shouted, whilst me and Rob looked at each other and sniggered, despite our earlier animosity.

"Did you dress this patient like this? And stop wailing, woman. He will be showered, and er, shaved, when he's been fully assessed."

Mind you, I noticed that he too stood in the corridor, issuing orders. Obviously another one wondering what the hell he was dealing with *this* time.

Jimmy was off the bed fully now and began trundling towards us zombie-like, arms stretched out in front of him, eyes wide and hair a quiver. With his gown flapping about him he looked like the Mummy Returns. We all took a step back, bumping into one another and fumbling to get to the back in case one of us had to make a decision. Suddenly a gentle voice behind took charge. We breathed a sigh of relief: reinforcements had arrived.

"Now, now, Jimmy. Let's just calm you down, eh? Come and sit back on this nice comfy bed for me, there's a good lad."

Huh? Gaz?!

Yes indeed. Gaz had stepped forward, got hold of Jimmy and was softly steering him back towards the bed. With an arm around the old guy's thin shoulders, he lowered him down gently onto the mattress so as not to aggravate his damaged ribs. I watched in silent fascination as Jimmy gazed at Gaz with watery blue eyes, mumbling to himself quietly as he allowed himself to be ushered back into the side room. Gaz sat down beside him and continued talking nonsense to the old fella until Jimmy was completely calm again. After a few minutes Gaz shut up, looked up at the rest of us and smiled.

"See? He's just a pussy cat really. You've just got to know how to handle him."

He patted Jimmy's thin arms and handed him a fresh drink of water. Jimmy sniffed it, pulled a face and grunted as if we had offered him rat poison. Of course, I don't think Jimmy knew what water actually looked or tasted like.

"Well, you obviously have the knack, Gaz," the doctor said with warm appreciation. "But then, he is, of course, your granddad. He obviously recognizes you above anyone else."

Will and I shared a look above the heads of the others and made polite sounds of agreement. And total disbelief. Who would have thought it of dopey old Gaz? Oh well, at least we'd found one thing he was good at.

"Could you just wait a little longer while we get him settled for the night then?" the doctor asked with a smile. Gaz seemed to grow a further three inches in height as he answered.

"Yeah. No problem, mate. Don't want the old guy to get upset again, do we?" By this time Jimmy had picked up a TV remote and was trying to play it like a mouth organ.

Nurse Bliss was explaining Gaz's heroics to Nurse Bridges who slinked up the corridor to us all. When she reached our little group, she leaned up to Gaz *and kissed him on the cheek!* At least he had the grace to blush and smile fetchingly as Will and I stood with our mouths open.

"Do you two want to go and sit in the waiting room while I er… finish off here?" he asked us, smirking ever so slightly.

We left him to it. Swine!

Chapter 11

It was quite dark by the time we three left the hospital. The night air was chilly and there was a thin mist rolling up from the river, but we were too engrossed in our recent acts of bravery and heroism to notice the cold. I left my nagging doubts about the whole Jimmy-thing in the hospital. I had decided that beating myself up for falling out with my best mate wasn't going to get us anywhere: after all, we all have our doubts from time to time, don't we?

Gaz was proudly wearing his badge of honour: well, a hand knitted, smelly old scarf that Jimmy had presented to him as his way of saying thanks to his "grandson" for all his help. Honestly, you'd think we'd just saved the world from nuclear Armageddon or put a man on Mars the way we were going on. I could already see us appearing on Panorama, well, YouTube at least. Rob had decided that we would probably qualify for the Queen's medal for gallantry or something, but Gaz simply wanted a kebab and a shower. This was odd – Gaz actually asking for a shower I mean. Rob questioned him closely.

"You feeling a bit scruffy then?" he asked.

"Yeah, I am actually. And my shoulders ache. Must be from hanging onto the old guy for all that time." He scratched his shoulder as he did so.

Rob and I exchanged a glance at each other and almost without realizing it stepped a little away from the hero of the hour.

"You did really well back there, mate," I told him, reaching out to pat him on the back, then realizing, and dropping my arm to my side again. I gave him a manic grin, to compensate.

"Cheers, Will, but we all did something to help Jimmy back there, didn't we?" He absentmindedly scratched his hair this time. Rob and I both clocked that gesture at the same time.

"Oh, I don't know about that," Rob replied, rubbing his left arm, the one nearest to Gaz. "I was a bit of a tit back there, wasn't I?"

He seemed quite ashamed of himself. His head was down, and he was sort of drooping along. I felt sorry for him.

"Yeah, you were, Rob, really, but you were being a tit with our best intentions at heart. *One* of us had to try to talk some sense some of the time."

My armpit suddenly felt all hot and prickly, despite the cool night air, and I reached inside my jacket to scratch it. "You know, we rely on you to be the voice of reason sometimes, mate," I continued, noticing the other two giving me quizzical looks.

I was thinking about my own reaction to being in that hospital again. It had taken all my nerves of steel (as if) and some help from my mate Rob to not run screaming into a wall on my demented dash out of the Emergency Department. Hardly the hero of the hour, was I?

We passed by the warm and inviting sights and sounds of the local McDonald's but none of us had any cash left so we just sniffed up the meaty smells as we walked on by. The door opened as someone came out, but we didn't look in too closely as that would have been even more of a torment. I was starving, I realized.

"But what happens now?" Gaz was asking of the two of us when our way ahead was blocked, like when the sun goes behind a huge black cloud. Puzzled, we drew to a halt and looked up. Mad Mick and Big Bird. We groaned in unison.

"Oh, look, Mick. My three best little mates. Shouldn't you three all be tucked up in bed by now?" Bernice was shovelling a greasy great burger into her mouth as she spoke to her beloved, but we got the message all right, as it dripped out through the fat and gristle.

"Yeah, together," offered Mick, through a mouthful of chips. They both cackled with laughter.

Rob was the first one to speak. I just stood there like a dummy whilst Gaz gazed at his hat, perched at a jaunty angle on Bernice's bonce.

"Yeah, yeah, very funny. Look, you two, we're not in the mood tonight. Do you mind?" And he moved to go around them, but the gruesome twosome simply stepped out together to block his way. I noticed that each one of them was broad of beam and that they were getting on for nearly six feet tall as they towered over us threateningly. Actually, I tried to recall a time when we had been this close to Mick, ever. I watched dully as he handed over his burger and chips to Bernice and moved to grab Rob by the front of his jacket, almost lifting him off the ground.

"You talking to me, you skinny little runt?'" he demanded, growling through clenched teeth. I felt my stomach flip for about the third time in as many hours. Here we go again, I thought.

Next, out of the fog that was beginning to swirl inside my head, I heard, "Oy, put him down lard arse, or I'll sock you one!"

Gaz, man! What are you thinking? I stared at him in disbelief, but so did Mick, as he dropped Rob down and turned towards Gaz.

Obviously, my mate's earlier acts of bravery had gone to his head. Bernice stood back, grinning with teeth like a horse, and put down their two meals to get a better view of the action which surely must follow. As she bent to put the food on a bench outside the shop, Gaz darted forward and grabbed his baseball cap off her head.

"And I'll have that back an' all," he told her, stuffing it inside his shirt. I heard Mick make a sound like a bull about to charge, before he lurched forwards like a Chieftain tank to protect his precious partner from further attack. He then grabbed Gaz and bodily lifted him off the ground, shaking him like a rag doll.

He had a fist raised, ready to belt the living daylights out of Gaz for his cheek, but Bernice stepped forward with a shifty look at the doorway to McDonald's. I realized she didn't want to cause too much of a scene outside one of their favourite meeting places. I mean, who would want to be barred from Maccy D's? She placed a meaty arm on Mick's bulging biceps as he lowered Gaz back to the pavement. Gaz was pale and shivered slightly but he maintained eye contact with his she-devil aggressor. I worried that he might turn to stone for that: she was the gorgon Medusa, especially now that she was no longer wearing Gaz's cap to hide her scraggy rats' tails hair. Stealthily I moved behind the two of them, edging out of their way.

"Ah, is diddums cold then?" she whined, breathing heavily into Gaz's frosty face. She gripped hold of Jimmy's scarf and twisted it tightly on his neck until Gaz started to turn a peculiar shade of purple. Still he stared her down. One or two customers came out of the restaurant then, coughing nervously as they sidled by. Mick sort of gurned at them, which was obviously supposed to signal – don't worry, we're just messing about – but which had the effect of causing the other customers to flee on their way with a worried expression.

Rob, I noticed, was sitting in the nearby flower bed where Mick had dropped him. He was looking shifty and slightly worried but not as frantic as the situation warranted, I thought. When Gaz started whistling and choking, Bernice loosened her grip, relieving him of the scarf passed on to him by the grateful Jimmy.

"I'll have that then, instead of the 'at," she told him, wrapping the warm but fairly grubby scarf around her double chins. Rob was staggering to his feet slowly. About time too, I was thinking, when he approached the two mutants with a sly grin.

"Ok you two; I think I know just what you both need."

Together they turned questioningly towards him, leaving Gaz to his own spluttering defences and ignoring quiet little me who had one eye on another prize. You see, we're a tag team, us three, and at least two of us had read each other's minds while all this was going on. I knew what was coming. Rob walked calmly up to Mick and Bernice and flung a handful of dust and dirt from the flower bed straight into their faces. At the same time, he grabbed the still struggling Gaz, telling me, "Come on, Will, quick, don't just stand there!"

I didn't need a second telling. As the two monsters bellowed and roared, trying to clear their eyes of coal dust, clarts and pigeon poo, I grabbed both of the still-warm McDonald's meals from the bench and took off after my friends. From the safety of the top of the hill I shouted down to them, "Goodnight, Shrek and Fiona! Thanks for the grub!"

We dug into the food hungrily, sharing it between us, as we ambled off home in the dark. What a night!

***

Back at home I wanted to dodge any questions from nosey Jilly, but she was so wrapped up in the boyfriend on the sofa that you couldn't quite tell where Jilly ended and Steve began. I peeped my head round the living room door, shuddered at the slurping noises and ran up to the bathroom two steps at a time, making vomiting noises all the way.

"I heard that," shouted Jilly, pausing for a moment to come up for air.

In the bathroom I had a good look at myself in the mirror. I was a sort of sickly grey colour, my hair was standing on end, and I noticed scratch marks around my neck. Hmm. I didn't remember either Bernice or Mick getting that close to me. I stripped my shirt off and looked more closely, leaning over the sink to peer at a couple of raised, red welts which were appearing on my chest and near my armpits. Oh God – the shock of all the night's action had brought me out in some kind of lurgy.

Then I really started to feel dizzy and faint. What if I had some awful disease brought on by stress? You read about things like that happening. I mean, some very normal people turned wacky when things went wrong for them. What was it called? Post Traumatic Stress Syndrome? What if all my hair fell out? I might even start lining up cutlery in the kitchen drawer, instead of just licking it and chucking it in, like I normally did.

I had the sudden compunction to scrub at my hands and started running the hot water. Now come on: that is just not normal, is it? Not when you're 15 and don't have a girlfriend. I scrubbed and scrubbed, using as much of Mam's glamorous liquid soap as I could fit into my cupped hands. It felt smooth, slippery and lovely, but I still felt scruffy and tainted. I kept remembering the dull thump of poor old Jimmy hitting the deck, the sounds of a boot against ribs, his mouth gasping for air like a fish out of water.

I reached up to turn on the shower, letting it run hot for a good ten minutes, like you do, when the bathroom door opened and there was Jilly. I don't know what, or who, I expected it to be really. I sat down on the side of the bath in relief.

"What?" she demanded. "Hurry up and get out of here."

She also must have thought I looked weird or freaky because she asked, more kindly than usual.

"What's the matter, face ache? You been eating bugs again?"

"I feel really weird, Jill," I told her. "Where's Mam?"

"Out with Dad and not back for ages yet. You know how upset she was earlier? Well Dad decided to take her to the cinema, try to cheer her up a bit. What's up?"

Ah, yes. I had noticed Mam being a bit quieter than normal today. She had been singing along to the radio, that programme where they play all the hits from years back, then she went quiet quickly after that. Something had obviously triggered a memory for her. Happy, or sad, I don't know.

Jilly looked more closely at me then, scanning my face and body for tell-tale signs of trouble. Her expression changed slightly; she looked 'softer' somehow, concerned about her little brother. Her *remaining* brother… now that Ross was gone.

"You haven't been sick in that sink, have you? I only cleaned it at tea-time." She smiled slightly, putting the back of her hand to my hot brow.

She peered into the sink, then leapt back and screamed at the top of her voice. I nearly passed out in fright, falling back into the bath, and lay there with my feet sticking up in the air, hot water soaking me. I bashed my head as well, but she wasn't bothered about that. She was jumping up and down, screaming blue murder when Steve burst through the door with a rolled-up, floral umbrella in his hand.

"What the…? Jilly, are you alright? What's he gone and done now?" he demanded, looking at me as menacingly as he could with a pink umbrella in his hand. Jilly stopped screaming and pointed to the sink. Steve peered in.

"What?" he asked.

"Oh, don't mind me, everybody," I began, trying to clamber out of the bath and turning off the shower. "I'll just knock myself senseless and get out of your way, shall I?"

I too stood over the sink then, dripping warm suds onto the floor.

"What?" I asked Jilly. Steve and I couldn't see what all the fuss was about. We shot a look at each other, wondering if she'd been eating too many goji berries again. My sister grabbed both of us by the back of our heads and forced our faces down towards the sink.

"Look, you morons!" she screamed, turning away from "it" in disgust. There was nothing there. A speck or two of muck washed from my hands perhaps; but then the specks moved. Or crawled, to be precise. Fleas!

Steve and I nearly knocked each other senseless to get out of that bathroom, I can tell you. Jilly grabbed the rolled-up umbrella and started bashing me over the head with it whilst Psycho Steve screamed like a girl, forcing me back inside.

Jill bellowed at me. "Will! Where the hell have you been tonight, and who with?"

Shielding my head with my arms I managed to mumble, "I was only out with the lads…"

My sister and her boyfriend slammed the door shut and leaned their bodies against it. She shouted at me from the landing.

"If you aren't in that shower, with all your clothes on, in two seconds, I'll come in and strip you!"

I winced at that, then smiled as I pictured the lads' faces when I told them that little nugget.

"Steve, go outside and light the barbecue," she demanded.

I cracked the door open a touch to see if she really was as batty as she sounded from inside the bathroom, but she screamed like a ninja and kicked it shut in my face.

"Jilly, you mad cow. What's the barbie for?" I demanded.

"To burn all your scraggy clothes, you little weasel!" she shouted. "Get them all off and throw them out of the window. I always said your friends were flea-bitten little mongrels. Now I know I was right all along."

I couldn't argue with that, now could I?

Later, sitting in the shed, smelling sweetly of my mam's very expensive bath bombs and our Jilly's birthday talc, I told Ross all about the night's events. Sitting in the old chair, pulled up close to the photo of my big brother, softly lit by the votive candles from St Peter's church, I finally felt safe, clean and secure again. I didn't tell my parents what had happened – they simply wouldn't get it. I was always worried about upsetting them too much, after everything they had been through in the last couple of years. I knew their inclination to over-dramatise simple events, and more importantly, they'd probably put me on a curfew and how would THAT solve the problems of Jimmy and Mad Mick? So, after my bath, I sneaked out down the garden to the shed.

I missed our Ross: my big bro, my hero. I'd always looked up to him. I missed hearing his loud laughter around the house. Actually, I missed the sound of *any* laughter around our house. Since we lost Ross, nobody ever laughs any more. Doors are closed now, tears flow behind them and in the shower, the radio or TV often drown out any sorrows and my parents talk in hushed voices and through clenched teeth.

My dad does his best, Jilly's quite good at taking my mam to a different, happier place, but life at home just isn't the same anymore. My mam has the look of a photograph that is slowly fading, losing its colour and definition. She's always been an attractive, extrovert sort of person, helping at our local church and around the community, but now she rarely goes out. She's developed a few wrinkles, her hair has lost its sheen, and her voice is now hard and brittle, where once it was soft and comforting.

I found a little flash of the mam I used to have just the other day, mind. I knew she'd had a bad morning and was trying to cheer herself up with her usual tactic – hoovering. I felt so bad about the way she was so often sad or distracted, so when I heard her getting the cleaning stuff out of the cupboard I leapt into action. Mam likes to tidy up to some classic rock tracks but hadn't put any sounds on today: a sure sign she needed a laugh. I grabbed Flora's wig, found a pinny on the back of the kitchen door and nicked some make-up from the bag Jilly left in the downstairs loo. Rolling my trouser legs up, and slipping into Jilly's high heels, I found the track I needed on my phone. As Mam went to dust the living room, I turned the Hoover on behind her, set play on my mobile, and shimmied about to Queen's classic track "I Want to Break Free".

At first, she leapt about three feet into the air, then she stood with her Marigolds and duster and laughed at me, open-mouthed. For a minute the two of us danced around the room, flicking at picture frames with dusters, tossing cushions about and mincing about like a couple of drag queens, before the track stopped and we both collapsed onto the settee in hysterics.

Coming up for breath, and wiping her eyes with a duster, Mam grabbed me into a headlock, before it turned into a soft, loving cuddle.

"Ohh, Will," she whispered into my hair. "You don't know how much I needed that!" She smiled. "Or how much I love you. Idiot." She grinned and kissed me on the cheek. "Now go and wipe that make-up off before Jilly sees it."

It felt great, I tell you. Warmed my heart. Because believe me, it doesn't happen often enough.

Quite a lot of the time I'm like the brother everyone forgot. Nobody will talk to me about Ross, about what happened to him, and I need them to. I really need them to! Sometimes I feel like I'm a pan about to bubble over. I need Jilly, Dad, or Mam to come and take me off the heat and say nice things until the bubbling subsides. But they don't: they can't. That's why my mates are so important. With them, I can be me, Will. I can tell a joke, knowing they'll react. I can give them a dead leg, or rugby tackle my pain and frustration out of them, and they'll take it like a man and still come back for more. Even having the dummies is a big help, a crazy distraction.

Thank God I have Ross in the shed. He can't contribute much, but he's a great listener, like he always was. He has a cheerful, friendly look on his face in the photo, which invites confidences and the sharing of secrets.

"Honestly, Ross, wait till I tell you what happened tonight," I begin. "You remember Jimmy Jesus…? Yep, that's the guy. Well, this evening, me and the lads…"

***

It took ages to get off to sleep. I was still tossing and turning when I heard my parents come home. I was trying to hear Jilly's rumblings of discontent from below in the living room but as my dad came upstairs all I could really hear was him going "Really?", "Shocking" and "Fancy that…" as he trudged wearily to bed. I smiled to myself in the dark. Dad had heard it all before and was a past master at making comforting noises at the right moment. One day last year I ran in with my hands covered in blood, well, tomato sauce actually, and told him I'd just assassinated the postman.

"Oh yeah, son. Why?" he had asked, not looking up from his newspaper.

"Because he tore my PC Geek monthly when he put it through the letter box," I told him, but he replied, saying, "Really? That's a shame. Well done, son".

Should I tell Dad about the situation with Jimmy? I wondered. I hoped that the old bloke was settled comfortably in hospital, probably sleeping like a baby – unlike me. He was hopefully dosed up to the eyeballs on nice floaty painkillers, warm and safe in a soft, clean bed. This had to be better than him lying on a bundle of rags in a shop doorway or behind the railway arches, topped up with Brown Ale and Meths like usual. But, what next for him? And, just as importantly, for us? How on earth were we going to adopt Jimmy now? Where was he going to live? What would we feed the old guy with? I'd never seen him at such close quarters and truly, I admitted it to myself and no-one else, he was a scary old guy. And I'd seen more of Jimmy than I ever thought any normal 15-year-old lad needs to see.

I closed my eyes and shuddered at the images I was struggling to shift from my mind. One day, we'll laugh about all this, I told myself.

An hour later, when the house was settled and quiet, I was still wide awake, worrying. Something was nagging at my brain, but I couldn't work out what it was. I'd giggled to myself at the thought of Bernice taking the scarf from Gaz. He'd got his cap back, but she thought she had won by taking the scarf from him in return. Well, she'd certainly picked up more than she bargained for there! I scratched my armpit in memory, reassured as I was that all known nasties had been either flushed down the shower or burnt on the barbie. Ah, I loved that shirt as well. Oh well, I remembered I had seen one very similar in the second-hand clothes shop me and the lads had been in… No, I couldn't. Could I?

Oh, this is ridiculous, I thought, glancing at the clock. One-fifty a.m. There was a strange creaking on the landing. Probably just the radiator settling cold, I told myself. Wonder if the lads are awake. Shall I text them? Better not. Jilly had ears like a fruit bat and could hear anything. She didn't need another excuse to come flying into my bedroom like the Jabberwocky, to fill me in.

There was that funny creak again, only this time it sounded like it was in my room. What the…? I lay there for a minute, holding my breath so I could hear more closely. When I could feel my lips turning blue and my face was like a beetroot I exhaled and lay there, nervously gazing around. Everything seemed normal in the room, as usual, though again I had the nagging feeling that something wasn't right. After everything we had been through tonight, I was feeling pretty paranoid, I can tell you.

I sat up to look around more closely, not bothering to put the bedside light on in case it woke the whole house. Well, come on, I'm pretty hard, me. What could happen to me here, in my own bedroom, in the dark, in the middle of the night?

Kylie was still hanging there, blowing me my very own personal little kiss. I blew one back at her. In the other corner, hanging from the curtain rail was my Eagle-Eyes Para-Action Man, suspended there in his net parachute for ever – well, since I was six. He was moving slightly I noticed. Must be a draught from somewhere, I thought.

Suddenly my eye was drawn to my bedroom door: did it just move open a bit? I froze in fear. Shit. Was there someone standing there, looking straight at me? I began to shake as I slid back down in the bed, clutching the sheets to my chin. Could Big Bird and Mick have got into the house to get their hideous revenge? Nah, I'd have heard them; or smelled them at least. My heart was beating loudly in my ears when the normal voice in my head told me what I was looking at. My dressing gown on the back of the door. Freak!

I leapt out of bed and in two hops had wrenched it down and leapt back in again. This was so I could look at the poster on the back of the door of the tennis girl scratching her bare bum. Well, she used to do that for me, until Jilly took revenge on me for using her false eyelashes as fishing bait: then she painted a pair of frilly knickers over the model's rather pert posterior. I didn't tell Jilly that it just added to my fantasy…

I had just calmed myself down enough to begin to think about sleeping when I swear the wardrobe door started to slowly creak open. I sat up again in the gloom and stared hard at it. I had convinced myself that I was imagining it when *a hand appeared from behind the wardrobe door!* Oh. My. God. I felt sick. It looked like a female hand too. Bernice? In my bedroom! I told myself to get a grip – she'd never fit in my wardrobe.

"Jilly?" I whispered. "Is that you?"

Nothing. The hand was slowly followed by an arm. Whoever it was in my wardrobe, at two o'clock in the morning, had had enough and was coming out to get me.

"Jilly, just get out of there, you fool," I told her, trying to control the wobble in my voice. "Look, I'm really sorry I gave you fleas, but there could be loads of the little buggers in there. You'll catch something. Please come out, Jilly."

I was pleading with her, praying to God that it was Jilly in my wardrobe.

All of a sudden, there was an unearthly scratching, squeaking sound and the wardrobe door burst open as two bodies tumbled out onto the floor. I screamed in terror and dived under the covers. Then there were lights snapping on, out on the landing, the sounds of my dad bellowing like a bear and my mam crashing into walls in her sleepy confusion. My door was flung open, there was the sound of an almighty crash and my light suddenly blazed on.

"Will...! What the...?"

My dad had fallen on top of Keith who was lying on top of Flora. It looked a bit like a mating session for garter snakes as their limbs twisted and twined in the bright light of my bedroom. In my worry and disgust at the various events of the last couple of hours, I had completely forgotten that I had stashed the two dummies in my wardrobe, when I had tidied the room up before going out. Jilly appeared at the door at that moment, twisty red rubber curlers in her hair and wearing Betty Boop pyjamas. She rubbed her eyes blearily before looking down in disgust at the scene on my floor.

"Eewww ... Dad..." she began.

"Don't even think about it, Jilly," he told her sternly, then glared at me as he hissed, "And you, Will. We'll talk about this in the morning."

He kicked both Keith and Flora hard, away from the door and slammed it shut. I got out of bed and stuffed Keith under my bed as best I could. His feet stuck out the end of the bed, but it would have to do. Flora I sat on the chair at my desk, straightening her wig as I did so. I thought about putting Facebook on to keep her occupied but decided against it. It was a bit late: most of my mates would be asleep. And anyway, I had another problem to sort out, but it would have to wait until morning. With a heavy heart I got back into bed, trying not to picture poor old Nigel, lying under a bush in someone's garden, in the cold and the dark, all alone.

I hope he hasn't been arrested, I thought.

Chapter 12

I had about three and a half hours of disturbed, boggle-minded sleep when my mobile went off with a chirpy little cheep: Rob, texting me at seven a.m. Thanks a bunch, mate.

"UthnkNige'sstll under his bush?"

Well, he hasn't sneaked back in during the night, I thought. Don't really expect to find him singing in our shower or eating a hearty breakfast in my kitchen. Poor old lad must be knackered by now, frozen solid and probably covered in creepy crawlies I should think.

I texted both Rob and Gaz to meet me as soon as possible, at the end of the street where we had stashed Nige when we had gone to rescue old Jimmy. I winced as I remembered what that poor old bloke had gone through, but now was not the time to dwell on it. Hopefully, Jimmy was sitting up in a nice warm hospital bed, clean shaven and eating porridge for breakfast, without a side order of cooking sherry. We had Nigel to rescue now, and he was at least equally as important as Jimmy. Well, a lot more fun, and a hell of a lot less trouble in the long run, I told myself.

My mam was calling to me to have some breakfast so I opened the fridge, grabbed a carton of milk and a piece of cold Tandoori chicken and dashed out of the back door before she could say Kellogg's.

It was a beautiful sunny and slightly frosty morning, one of those days when it's good to be alive. I sauntered off down the road eating my chicken and drinking my milk when I realized I was being followed by my cat, Cooking Fat (don't ask), and next door's dog, Bert. They were good friends who often went for walks together. I stooped to stroke them both and carried on my way but stopped at the end of our road. They were both still behind me, C.Fat up on the fences and Bert wagging along placidly at my heels with a silly grin on his face.

"Ok, you two – enough. Bog off. I've got serious business to attend to and you two will just get in the way. Go on. Push off," I told them – sternly, I thought. C.Fat simpered and arched his back and Bert just sat there, gazing expectantly at my chicken.

I glanced at my watch, sighing. I didn't have time to take both of them back to their houses, but I had to get rid of them or they'd never give up. I couldn't face the thought of them getting run over or becoming lost. I'd never live it down in my house and would get the blame, even though both of these animals could work things out better than… well, better than Gaz actually. If ever there was an intelligence test between me and Gaz and C.Fat and Bert, my money would be on the cat and dog, believe me. Rob could tip the balance our way though.

I tore off another piece of chicken and the two of them sat up, rather like soldiers standing to attention. Aha. I pulled off a tiny little bit and threw it as far as I could into old Mrs Master's garden. Together they dashed off over her fence and began snuffling about in her undergrowth. Ha – they'll never find it in there, I laughed to myself as I legged it down the street, past the garages and round the corner. And they'll never find me either cos they don't know where I'm going.

I smirked as I put my chicken bone in a bus stop rubbish bin, some way down the street. Can't be too careful, don't want rats in our nice area; then drained the contents of the milk carton. I was just putting that in the bin too when from behind me I heard a combined "Mieowruff". I don't believe it: Bert and C.Fat! They'd taken a short cut through all the gardens and had cut me off. Bugger. Who said animals were dumb?

I plodded on dejectedly, deciding to ignore my companions as best I could.

Three streets later I had lost my two funny little friends and had picked up another couple on the way. Gaz and Rob. They looked remarkably chipper I can tell you. They had both slept fine, clear consciences, no doubt. Or rather, no naked dummies and dads tumbling about on their bedroom floor. I told them the story as we walked, keeping them entertained until we reached the street where we thought we'd left Nigel.

"Oh man, you should have filmed it," Gaz began. "You could have earned a fortune on Tik Tok!"

"Oh dear, if only I'd thought of that," I told him sarcastically.

We had stopped at the point where we thought we'd left Nigel, but in sunlight, and without a stinky old tramp in our sights, it looked quite different. We gazed around. The houses were mostly large, set back from the road with neat, well-tended gardens. There was a council office housed in an old Victorian building and a doctor's surgery, but we decided to start looking for Nige under hedges and bushes.

We split up, so as not to look too suspicious to any passers-by or residents. Rob sauntered to the far end of the road, and Gaz and I took opposite sides at our end. I had only looked under one hedge when I heard Gaz calling, quietly. "Here, Nige, come on, boy."

And there was me thinking he'd begun to act in a grown-up manner last night, I thought, straightening up.

"Oy, Gaz man," I called quietly. "Are you expecting him to answer? He's a dummy," I reminded him.

Gaz stopped stooping and calling and looked at me in a perplexed way.

"Is there something wrong, Will?" he asked, questioningly.

I shook my head. "No, no, mate. You just carry on."

Further down the road I could see Rob on all fours, peering under a hedge. He whistled quietly and gestured for me and Gaz to catch up to him. Looking about carefully, we tried to approach him in a casual manner but probably looked as if we were casing the joint, getting ready to burgle one of these houses. I reached up to turn Gaz's cap on the right way then remembered the previous owner and dropped my hand with a shudder. We reached Rob and dropped down to the ground beside him.

"Look, in there," he mouthed.

Peeping under the hedge I could see Nigel, still lying where we'd left him. He was further into the garden than I remembered, lying flat on his back with his grey cotton wool hair sticking up on his head. He looked a bit damp and shiny, probably covered in dew.

"Let me see," asked Gaz. He stuck his head through, losing his cap in the privet hedge in the process.

"Yep, that's him," he declared, as if we were in any doubt, then he stuck his head back through and started calling, "Nige. Oy, Nigel. Over here, mate."

Rob and I grabbed him by the shoulders and hauled him out of the hedge.

"Gaz – give over! What sort of place is this anyway? Have another look," I told him, shoving him face first into the hedge again. Beside me Rob was shaking with laughter. I gave him a withering look.

"It says, 'Happy Valley Retirement home: We're here for as long as you are'. And it's all quiet, at the moment," Gaz told us, coming back into view on the street, hair on end and full of twigs.

"Right," began Rob, taking charge. "We'll go in up the drive, like proper people do. We'll grab Nigel and get out of there pretty quick."

We were just rounding the corner of the hedge when we heard the sound of a wheelie bin being trundled out of a side door. Diving back where we had just come from, we looked at each other in alarm. Rob poked his head round the corner to have a quick look.

"Well? Who is it?" I asked.

"It's an old granny, probably aged about 80," he told us.

"Oh, that's ok then. You jump on her and overcome her, and me and Will can grab Nige before she can do anything," Gaz told us, setting his cap firmly back on his head.

"Gaz – she's at least 80 years old!" Rob told him, looking shocked.

"What? You think it might take all three of us to hold her down?" he asked incredulously. I hit him. I had to. Rob peeped up the drive again.

"She's leaning on the bin, gasping for breath. She shouldn't be doing that at her age," he told us.

Gaz looked concerned. "Well, if she stops, she'll die," he told Rob witheringly, like Rob was the stupid one.

"No, I mean she shouldn't be wheeling the bin… oh never mind. Look, Will. You go and help her with the bin, and me and Gaz will run in and get Nigel. Ok?"

It was a simple, but brilliant plan. What could go wrong?

I set Gaz's cap on the right way again and the three of us started to make our way up the drive. Before we could get within calling distance of the old dear, however, she started trundling past us, eyes peering dimly towards the garden and the hedge, where Nigel lay on the grass. I stepped out in front of her, to cause a distraction. She seemed to not see any of us and waddled on, pushing her glasses further up her nose, little fat legs and wrinkly stockings marching unsteadily on.

"Alf, is that you? What on earth are you doing out here? You'll catch your death," she declared in a shaky voice, heading towards Nigel. Oh no. I could see at once where this was going.

Rob beat me to her, catching hold of her arm and trying to turn her towards him.

"No, no, it's ok. It's not Alf. Come on back inside and we'll rustle you up a nice cup of tea."

He tried to lead her back towards the home as Gaz and I ran forward to grab Nige by his arms and legs. The old dear was mumbling about not being allowed to sunbathe or wear a hankie on your head when it's hot, when two windows opened upstairs and another voice was heard.

"Oy, you lot. What do you think you're up to?" said the first, younger voice.

"Alf? You all right, mate? What have they done to you?" demanded another, elderly male voice. "Here, Mildred, someone's trying to take old Alf away again," he continued, his voice fading as he spoke to someone in the room with him.

"Oh, for God's sake…" Rob began, nodding to us two to hurry up and get Nige. A window was pushed open wider.

"I'm ringing the Poliss, mind!" an old voice called.

Rob had led the old dear to a side door, telling her firmly it was NOT Alf on the lawn and that it was my granddad and I had come to take him home. She twisted her hands, looking uncertainly at him as Gaz and I started running with Nigel's body. We were almost at the gate with him when one of his legs dropped off. The old dear screamed.

"See! I knew it was him! Alf! Alfred! Are you ok? Don't worry – the Police are coming. Kick 'em with your good leg, mate."

By this time, we were away up the road, lugging bits of Nigel with us. Gaz had the dummy's head in one hand, whilst me and Rob carried his floppy body. We left one leg on the lawn near the gate. I was distraught. The poor old guy was going to be disabled! What was I going to tell Keith and Flora?

Ten minutes later we were sitting on my wall, Nigel put back together, mostly, sitting in between us all, laughing about what had just happened. I was grinning, but inside I felt bad that Nigel was now deformed. He was like a *real* old bloke now – he couldn't walk the same anymore.

"Do you think we'll end up as batty as that?" Rob asked, swinging Nigel's empty trouser leg. I glanced at Gaz, who had his hand behind Nigel's head, turning it to look at us individually as we talked.

"Some of us are already there, mate," I told him.

"Oh look, here's your Foo…I mean, Cooking Fat." Gaz said, reaching out to scratch the cat with Nigel's hand as he jumped purring onto the wall to join us.

"Hey you, where've you been?" I asked him, smoothing out his whiskers. Next thing we heard was a muffled "Woof" and the three of us turned to see Bert trotting up the street with Nigel's leg in his mouth.

"Bert – my hero!" I declared, jumping off the wall to greet him. Who said animals were dumb?

We were fussing over Bert, praising him for being such a wonder-dog, laughing about whether they might have discovered the real, one-legged Alfred safely tucked up with a cup of tea and a currant bun, when a deep brown voice from behind startled us.

"Aha, so it *was* you three, causing mayhem again back there," the voice declared.

We jumped to attention, like soldiers in front of their sergeant major, Rob holding Nigel's leg behind his back. Gaz stuffed the dummy's head up the front of his hoodie, where it bulged obscenely, like an alien about to explode out of him. I stepped in front of him. Our eyes flashed from one to another; were we about to be rumbled? Was this the end of our fun?

Rob spoke up, rather too brightly, I thought.

"Father O'Rafferty! How nice to see you."

He smiled. "How are you?"

The tall priest seemed to raise himself up to his full six feet four and grinned back down at us three oiks. He was a magnificent specimen – if you can say that about a man of the cloth. The lads were always happy to see him, unless it was inside the church at 9.30 on a Sunday morning like, or in Assembly in school.

I, of course, had started to tremble. This lovely guy brought back too many memories for me. And he knew it. He always went out of his way to be especially nice to me. The lads knew it too, coughing quietly and glancing at me protectively. I raised my eyebrows to them in response, silently telling them, *it's ok, guys, I can handle this today with you two by my side.*

Fr O'Rafferty smiled at us, hooking his hands into the belt of his jeans, and swaying back on his feet a little, a gesture I recognized as being an invitation to relax and be at ease in his presence, not a threat.

"I was just in the retirement home, checking on one of my parishioners, and wondered who was causing so much of a stir." His smile broadened, perfect teeth gleaming whitely.

I stepped forward. "Ah, well you see, Father, we had misplaced something and were just looking to see if it was in their gardens. We weren't making trouble – honestly."

Gaz was gurning at him – well, smiling really, and stepped forward to add his two pen'orth. I shook my head at him. It was probably not such a good idea, I was thinking. Just stand easy, Gaz.

"We thought that old lady was getting away, Father," he told the priest. "We didn't want her to run onto the road, so we grabbed her," he informed him.

Rob and I spun on Gaz.

"No, Gaz, we *got hold of her arm gently* and steered her back to the side door," Rob told him sternly. "We didn't grab her, Father, honestly," he told the priest, earnestly.

I was still a bit dumbstruck, to be honest. Father O'Rafferty grinned at the three of us, shaking his head genially.

"Guys, guys, it's ok, honestly. The elderly people on the top floor loved all the excitement. They're still chuckling about it in there. Really. Don't worry. You gave them all something to talk about."

I felt the release of breath from the three of us. We were like balloons deflating. I was finally able to smile again. We weren't going to be dragged to the Police. Or the Bishop. Or worse, our parents. Father O'Rafferty continued, folding his arms in front of him.

"I'm glad I caught you three. A little bird told me you might be just what I'm looking for."

We raised our eyes to him, suspiciously at first. What little bird would that be, I wondered. And how could we three numpties help this big bloke? We stepped forward.

"I'm holding a parish event," he began. My hackles began to rise, almost unconsciously. Church? Us three? "I need three handsome, attractive and confident mannequins for the catwalk, to strut their stuff and bring a touch of glamour to the proceedings."

Was he taking the mick? How could he have found out about the dummies? Gaz stepped forward.

"Mannequins, Father? And why did you think of us?"

The priest gazed at me directly. "Well, I was talking to your mam, Will. After I saw you the other day, I bumped into her and your sister in the supermarket."

"Jilly," we three said in unison.

"Yes, the lovely Jilly. I told her about the fashion show we're holding. Told her I had loads of girls volunteering for the catwalk, but that I was short on male models. She said you three would be perfect. Said you had exactly what I needed to bring some life and fun to the event."

"Male models?" I questioned him, stepping closer.

"And you have loads of *girls* already booked as models, you say, Father?" Rob asked, interested now.

"And would we have to share a dressing room with them though, Father?" Gaz prompted, too eagerly I thought.

We gave him a dig, me and Rob, one of us on each side of him.

"What?" he demanded, nudging us back. "I'm just thinking of Keith and Nige, that's all," he told us, shaking his head and gazing up at the priest.

As he spoke, Nigel's head slowly but surely worked its way out of his jumper and landed at the feet of the priest. Father O'Raff smiled and nudged it with one of his huge feet. I bent down quickly to grab it. Rob tried to divert his attention away from it.

"So, what sort of fashion are we talking about here, Father? Not old granny stuff, is it?" he asked, obviously thinking back to the second-hand shop visit we had made.

"Not at all, lads," the priest smiled, "the best in modern fashion for my models. Designer stuff for the girls, sports gear for the male mannequins. And look at you three – just what we need!" And he patted the top of Nigel's head.

But we had stopped listening after the words 'designer stuff for the girls…'. Even Nigel's head, nestling comfortably against my stomach, seemed to be looking instantly more interested and animated.

"Tell you what, guys. Why don't you drop into St Peter's one evening, and I'll fill you in properly?" He grinned at us. Beside me Gaz gulped. He's thinking about all those girls, half undressed, I thought, giving him yet another dig.

"We will!" Rob told the priest, in what I thought was a pretend Irish accent, so I gave him a dig as well. "See you soon, Father," and he started walking away with a spring in his step.

At the corner, I stopped my friends and gazed questioningly at them.

"Really, Rob. Are we going for this?" I asked him. "I mean… it's church, it's Father O'Rafferty and loads of elderly people. Again."

Rob turned his excited gaze on me. "Aye, Will. But it's also girls, beautiful ones, smart clothes, a lot of fun for our three dummies. We can make ourselves so useful at this fashion show. You know, carrying and fetching for the models, helping them, getting them drinks, finding their shoes and bags for each outfit. It's perfect. What do you think, Gaz?" he asked, turning to our other friend. Gaz had gone quite pale at the thought of it all. In fact, he looked like he was going to pass out.

"You ok, mate?" I asked him, feeling a bit concerned. "We'll go to St Peter's and find out more at least, eh?"

Gaz stopped in his tracks, shaking his head. "Not me, lads, no way," he mumbled, shaking his head.

Rob and I exchanged a puzzled look over his head. What? I mouthed at Rob.

"You mean, you don't want to talk to Raff about this, Gaz?" asked Rob. "You don't want to find out more?"

Gaz stood his ground, still looking shocked.

"Are you both daft?" he exclaimed. "He said he's going to fill us in! Have you seen the size of his muscles?"

Rob and I slapped him on the back and dragged him on, chuckling as we went.

Chapter 13

A week is a long time to decide on a plan, I've discovered. Honestly, you'd think we'd all joined MI5 or something the way the lads went on, clamming up as soon as an oldie drew near. Parents, sisters, school, all got in the way of us three getting together to come up with something foolproof and cunning to bring Bernice and Mick some retribution for their constant bullying of us. Rob had a couple of away footy games for the school team, Gaz had to have a couple of days in bed – well, on the lav actually – because of something he'd eaten. What, our Gaz, eating something weird? Never. It was probably an item of roadkill he'd found in his mam's fridge. Sorry, I mean, 'home-baked pie'. I was going to blame our Jilly's little cakes but decided life was too short, and we had serious business to attend to; we had to find a way of getting revenge on Bernice and Mad Mick for the trouble they brought to our lives. As Jimmy was safely tucked up in hospital for the foreseeable, we decided to give him some space to heal without drawing too much attention to ourselves. Personally, I was enjoying the break from Jimmy, and yes, I felt bad about that. I felt like I was letting the side down. And Jimmy didn't care, did he? He didn't care for hospitals either, it turns out...

After a week of frantic texting, swapping notes in History detention one night, and a quick gossip session behind the gym one break, we decided we knew exactly how we would bring about the downfall of those two thugs. Well, maybe not *exactly* how to do it, but we had a rough idea, and that was enough to spur us on. We were itching to get our own back. Saturday night couldn't come along quickly enough for us. We were giddy with anticipation.

In the meantime, however, we had decided we would go and talk to Father O'Rafferty about this up-and-coming fashion show. Obviously, I had some major concerns about going back into St Peter's church; I hadn't been there, or in *any* church, since Ross' funeral.

My mam and Jilly had started going back quite regularly, but I know that, at first, it was an ordeal for them. My dad didn't want to go at all, but he never really was a Believer in the first place. I think he was relieved that Mam and Jill were settling back into some kind of normality though. I could have a major attack of the heebie-jeebies just thinking about it, but Rob had convinced me that, once inside, if I concentrated on a tantalizing image of Fiona Bridges, wiggling down the catwalk in a pair of Kylie gold hotpants, I would be absolutely fine.

"Is that not totally sacrilegious, Rob?" I asked him. "Or blasphemous, or something equally damning?"

Rob had stopped in front of me, placed his hands on my shoulders and told me solemnly, "Will, mate, you're not going to Heaven anyway, so stop stressing about it."

We had arranged to meet Gaz on the corner near the church. We knew he would be a bit late because he had texted to say his mam had spotted Jimmy in the town centre, not far from the park, and he wanted to go to make sure it really was him, and not some other random old homeless bloke. I mean, really? How many were there hanging around our city centre, looking, smelling, and acting like our very own Jimmy Jesus? We knew he had escaped from the hospital after the attack, and that he had been reported everywhere from KFC bins (quite possibly him), a posh hotel on the sea front (probably not), behind a mosque (Jimmy?), and in Dooley's yard again (defo Jimmy.)

Rob decided Keith needed to come with us to see Father O'Rafferty, to add some kudos to the event and to convince the priest that he would be the star of the show. We decided not to take Flora because she may get jealous at the competition between herself and the beautiful Fiona and the other models. We'd ask Fr O'Raff his opinion on that.

Keith had been especially dolled up for this occasion and was looking pretty dapper, I thought. He was wearing one of my dad's golfing jumpers, a pair of smart jeans, some trainers my nan got for me which didn't actually fit me, and one of Jilly's smart navy-blue coats. She thinks that's still hanging in Mam's wardrobe... first up, best dressed in our house. I had insisted on washing Keith's face and hands but ignored Rob's suggestion that we clean his teeth. Honestly. He was wearing some after-shave though, just in case. I mean, to go to church you have to be presentable. We're not scruffs, you know.

It was evening time. There wasn't that much traffic in the city centre, just the odd bus rumbled past us, crossing the bridge towards the sea. One or two older people came out of the church but took no notice of us three sitting on the wall outside. St Peter's is a huge old place, right in the city centre, and built of a sort of honey-coloured stone. It's a majestic building, the sort of place which deserves respect when you walk past it on your way to the theatre or the park. I hadn't given it much thought since we lost Ross, but sitting there, in the soft evening air with the seagulls calling overhead, I felt a sort of curiosity building inside of me: almost a *need*. Maybe it was just a type of terror growing in me. Maybe I should just turn and run away, back over the bridge, towards the beach? Just keep on running. But, I reasoned, I had my mates at my side; I could do this.

Gaz appeared round the corner with a giant packet of crisps being held up to his mouth as he hoovered up the very last crumbs. So intent was he on this task that he walked straight into a lamppost, which shuddered and rocked with a metallic clang, leaving the passengers on a passing bus gazing at him in despair and amusement. Straightening his cap and rubbing his nose, Gaz approached us in his usual sloppy saunter.

"Hey, You Guys!" he sang, in the style of the Goonies, reaching out to high-five myself, Rob and Keith as we sat on the wall. Sometimes Gaz is just a little too much like that character Sloth, from the Goonies, for my liking. Keith promptly fell backwards and his head rolled off.

"Gaz, man – idiot! Watch it," I told him sternly, as I retrieved the head and tried to fix it back onto Keith's neck.

"Soz, Will," he responded, stuffing the crisp packet into his pocket. "I was too busy thinking about Jimmy. And of course, I see Keith as one of us lads. I was happy to see him there with you and Rob. Felt natural," he shrugged, straightening Keith's snazzy golf jumper.

"Did you find any sign of Jimmy then, Gaz? Was it him your mam saw?" Rob asked him, standing Keith up and linking arms with him so he didn't fall again.

"He's got a bruise on his cheek now," Gaz told us sorrowfully.

"What? Has he been attacked again, do you think?" Rob demanded hotly.

I was shocked and upset at this news about the old guy. The sooner we found Jimmy and put our Citizenship project into action the better, I thought, morosely. Oh yes, Project Jimmy was definitely on again. Rob was quite insistent on that.

Gaz pointed to Keith, gesturing with a finger that smelled strongly of Doritos.

"Not Jimmy – him, Keith. Look," then he licked his finger and went to rub at the dummy's face where a dark smudge had appeared.

"Oy, get your dirty hands off our clean Keith," I told him, firmly. Taking a tissue out of my pocket, I wetted it slightly in my mouth and gently cleared the scuff mark off Keith's cheek.

"There, good as new," I told the lads, glaring at Gaz.

"My nan used to do that to me, when I was little." Rob smiled.

"My nan still does," Gaz began, then looked at Rob and I as we laughed. "What?"

"Come on, you lot. Let's do this," I told them, and we made our way into St Peter's.

There's a shady, peaceful vestibule as you go through the main door from the street. Inside, we paused, glancing at leaflets for Cafod, first Holy Communion photographs, a list of readers and altar servers. There was very little noise; all was peaceful and calm, just the soft sound of traffic shushing by on the street outside. I glanced nervously at the lads, and they watched me closely, making sure I wasn't going to keel over, or make a run for it. Gaz wandered forward, leaving Rob and I to hold up Keith between us. He stopped further down the hall, in front of a statue of the Virgin Mary. We watched as he took his cap off, leaving his hair sticking up like Stan Laurel's. He was gazing at the statue as though he'd never seen it before, even though there's one just like it in our school reception.

Moving to stand alongside Gaz, Rob asked him, "You ok, mate?"

Gaz stepped back, taking in the whole statue in front of him. There was a slight smell of sweet incense in the air, and lots of soft candles glowing at her feet.

"Whoa…" He breathed. "Lads, look at her face."

Rob and I did as Gaz asked. The three of us, and Keith, stood quietly in front of the statue for a minute or two. An elderly parishioner came out of the door and whispered softly in our direction. "Well, look at you lovely young men. You should be very proud of yourselves, you four." Then she shuffled out of the main entrance.

"What's wrong with her face?" I asked Gaz, staring at the statue's serenely soft gaze, illuminated by candlelight.

"Shouldn't she be leaping up and down, screaming?" Gaz asked in quiet puzzlement.

Rob stood to face him, tearing his eyes from the statue to look at our friend.

"And just why should she be doing that?" he asked gently, with a look on his face which clearly said he really didn't want to know the answer.

"Well, she's standing on a snake, for starters," Gaz exclaimed in horror. Rob, Keith and I looked at the feet of the Virgin Mary. Sure enough, she was, and it was squirting blood and squirming.

Rob sighed. "Of course she is. That's not just a snake, Gaz; that's the devil himself."

Gaz jumped back, knocking into me and Keith. I grabbed his head again – just in case. Keith's, I mean, not Gaz's.

"See!" he exclaimed, still in hushed tones. Rob and I pushed him away from the statue and into the body of the church. "She should be leaping about, having hysterics," he hissed back at us, as if we were the thickos.

I noticed Keith eyeing the statue of Our Lady with quiet interest and wondered what was going through his mind at that moment. Were they communicating telepathically, I pondered? Was she passing on a secret message to Keith, maybe telling him to keep me safe and steady? After all, being who she was, she knew my inner turmoil. I grabbed Keith, and with Rob's help we moved on.

Pausing at the inner door to the church, Rob and I both automatically reached for the little holy water font to make the sign of the cross; old habits die hard, I thought. We exchanged a conspiratorial glance, then leapt forward together to stop Gaz from dipping his grubby Doritos fingers into the same holy water. He tutted at us, wiped his hand on his jeans and walked quietly forward, into the church, eyes agog.

St Peter's church is pretty majestic inside, as well as out. We stood together, the four of us, in hushed wonder, silently gazing about. There was the scent of flowers, wafting forwards from the main altar, delicately filling the air and mingling with the hint of incense and candle wax. I was aware of Rob beside me inhaling deeply. Icons of saints glowed in the light of many small votive candles, throwing flickering shadows onto alabaster faces, making them seemingly move and murmur, as if in silent prayer. Coloured stained glass windows cast jewelled patterns on the ancient, tiled floor, and somewhere up above us an organ played quietly, soft sounds rising and falling all around us. One or two parishioners were kneeling near the altar, unaware of, or uninterested, by us standing at the back. My stomach started to twist itself in knots, remembering a coffin covered in flowers and cards in front of that same altar, family members weeping in those very same front seats.

Suddenly, alongside of us, Gaz breathed out one quiet word.

"Jesus."

Glancing at our mate, we watched as he tilted his head back to take in the huge crucifix hanging above the altar, all that pain and glory evident in his near nakedness. Gaz looked quite pale in this half-light, with coloured shadows flickering across his face. Even Keith seemed in awe of this vision in front of us.

"Yep, that's him," Rob announced quietly. "The man himself." Then turning to me he asked softly, "You ok, Will? If it gets too much, just leave. Go and sit outside, mate."

I must admit I was feeling a bit shuddery by this point, but a door was opening at the far side of the altar, and a very tall, dark figure was emerging and making his way towards us. Gaz had sat down heavily in his seat as Father O'Rafferty made his smiling way forwards. Us three, I mean me, Rob and Keith, seemed to sort of stand to attention, although I was aware that my knees were shaking.

"Cor," whispered Gaz, "I'm not sure who has the most commanding presence in here," he told us quietly, nudging us and nodding at the priest, then pointing up at the figure of Christ above the altar.

"Gaz, man, give over," I hissed, narrowing my eyes at him.

"You'll get struck down for that," Rob told him with a smile.

Gaz sort of smirked at us, but before the priest reached us, the whole church started shaking as a loud rumble shuddered through the entire building. Gaz made a grab for the pew he was sitting at, his eyes wide, one hand clutching his chest.

"What's happening?" he squeaked in alarm. "Am I being struck down? What the…"

The tall figure of Father O'Rafferty was by our side then, looking at Gaz's stricken expression with delight.

"I take it you haven't been in St Peter's before then, Gaz?" he asked in his soft voice. Rob and I simply smiled and shook our heads at the priest.

"It's the trains, Gaz," Fr Raff told him patiently. "They run right underneath the church. Didn't you know that?"

I'd actually forgotten that fact myself. The rumble of passing trains had proved to be unnerving at Ross's funeral, but had then turned out to be a welcome distraction from the familial pain and distress of the occasion. Of course: the bridge outside took the trains across the river, away north to Newcastle, or back into the central station in town.

Gaz smiled up at the priest. "God, Father," he started, as I winced a bit at his choice of greeting, "I thought my time had come there for a minute. Phew, trains in a church, eh? Who would have thought it?" Father O'Rafferty didn't seem offended in the least. He simply grinned at our mate, who then stated, "Might have dislodged your man up there, all that passing traffic. Could have done him a mischief," nodding up at the hanging crucifix.

As Rob and I groaned in embarrassment, Fr Raff noticed Keith.

"And who would this be, eh, lads? Your handsome friend there?"

Rob held Keith firmly as I pushed him forward into a very formal bow, then we held out his hand for Fr O'Rafferty.

"Keith, this is Father O'Rafferty. Father, this is Keith, one of our mates and as you can see, a male model and perfect for the fashion show," Rob told the priest with a grin.

To our complete delight, he took Keith's proffered hand, shook it gently and bowed back at him.

"Lads, please, call me Raff," he told us in his gentle, lilting voice, "everyone else does." Then he looked very pointedly in my direction. "You ok, Will?" he asked, concern creasing his face and crinkling his eyes. I sort of gulped at him, nodding. I was finding it difficult to form words for some reason. Gaz jumped into the rescue, throwing me a quizzical look.

"Great place you've got here, Raff," he told the priest animatedly. "Is this where you're holding the fashion show then?"

Rob and I gave him a withering look. "Gaz, you don't really hold fashion shows inside churches," began Rob. "It's more like weddings and baptisms, and funerals..." then he realised and paused, blushing. I could still feel my knees knocking, and my breath was becoming a bit shaky too. What was this? What was happening to me? I felt like I was coming apart at the seams and didn't want to embarrass myself in front of the lads and Raff.

"Aha, and I hear you have another couple of 'friends' who could help out at the fashion show too," began Raff, putting a gentle hand on my shoulder and sitting me down in the pew beside Gaz. He gave me a friendly squeeze, before standing up and saying to the lads, "Why don't I show you some of the clothes that have already arrived, eh guys? They're in a room at the back. Let's leave Will to keep an eye on the church for a minute, eh?"

He gazed at me kindly as the lads stood up with some excitement.

His quiet consideration was making me worse, not better. I was really starting to let go now. Something was headed my way, as if from a great distance, coming in waves to wash over me, to knock the stuffing right out of me. I gulped and nodded, as the lads moved away with Raff, looking back to check I really was ok with them leaving.

I closed my eyes, remembering the flowers in this church, the coffin, my mam sobbing quietly into my dad's shoulder, Jilly walking with her head down, shoulders heaving. And me? Me, just numb, silent, staring at my brother's coffin, whilst inside my head I was screaming – "Ross! Ross… *Why?*"

Keith had been left in the pew beside me, "to keep me company," Gaz had said as he walked off with the other two. Without being held from both sides, he sort of tilted in towards me, and I found myself supporting the dummy on my right shoulder. Or was he supporting me? He felt like a mate. He felt like, despite his cold, hard body, he could feel my pain and discomfort at being in this church. His silence was a great relief, but it didn't stop my torment from bubbling up and spilling out. Grabbing hold of Keith's left hand, I gazed up at the crucifix, then I closed my eyes and sobbed, tears streaming unchecked down my face. And, finally, it was a bit of a relief to let them flow.

Chapter 14

After my fallout inside the church, I had left the lads and Keith and legged it home.

I had staggered into the kitchen, heaving for breath, sweating and shaking. I flopped down at the kitchen table, sniffing and snivelling, red faced and distressed. Jilly was inside our walk-in pantry, searching for something, and she'd heard me come in. Without sticking her head around the door, she shouted out to me, "Will, I can smell you from here! If you've been running away from somebody – again – can I suggest you run straight into the shower? Stinky little maggot," she added, for effect.

I couldn't even raise a smile. I simply sniffed into my sleeve and flopped my head down onto the kitchen table.

After a minute or two, I became aware of the kettle being switched on and a plate of biscuits was slid in front of me. Jilly sat opposite me, remaining silent, for a change, and simply waited. I raised my tearstained face to hers, sat up and shuddered quietly.

"Where've you been, Will?" my sister asked gently. "Have you been beaten up by Mad Mick again?"

I shook my head.

She continued, questioning me quietly. "Is it Jimmy? Has *he* been beaten up again?"

I shook my head, not trusting my voice to work properly yet. Jilly stood up as the kettle clicked off and began opening cupboards, getting cups out, calmly and in control. With her back to me as she made drinks she said, "You can tell me, you know, Will. I'll help if I can. Where have you been?"

Picking up a Jaffa Cake from the plate, I told her in a small gruff voice, "St Peter's."

Jilly paused, teaspoon in hand, and turned to face me with her eyebrows raised. "You've been in St Peter's?" she asked, incredulous. "By yourself?"

I picked bits of chocolate off the Jaffa Cake, letting them fall onto the table in front of me. Jilly would normally have gone ballistic at that simple act. I sneaked a look at her, gave a shuddery sigh, and told her, "No, the lads came as well. I think they're still there, with Raff…"

My sister leaned back against the sink, folded her arms, and stared at me with softer eyes than she would normally use for me. "And you couldn't hack it," she said, not unkindly. "It's your first time in there since we lost Ross, isn't it, Will?"

She placed a mug of hot chocolate in front of me and came to sit on the chair opposite from me, taking a biscuit for herself. Jilly gave a deep sigh. "You want me to get Mam?" she asked. I shook my head. My mam had had her fill of tears and tantrums this last year. I couldn't upset her further. "Shall I get your friends here?" she asked. Now I *knew* she had a heart: our Jilly offering to bring my mates to the house! Again, I shook my head, and was about to wipe my nose on my sleeve when a piece of kitchen roll was thrust into my hand.

"You know what you need?" Jilly told me, sitting back in her chair. "Go to the shed, Will," she continued. "Go and talk to Ross. Tell him how upset you are. He'll listen. He might not be able to help, but just saying it out loud helps a bit, you know."

I thought about this for a minute, taking a sip of the sweet chocolate drink, feeling the comfort of the warm cup in my hands. *Maybe she's right*, I thought.

"Go on," she continued, "I'll make sure nobody interrupts you."

I gave her a watery smile, then picked up my cup and made my way out of the back door and down the garden path, wiping my eyes and nose as I went, hiccupping slightly.

The shed was in darkness as I opened the door. I struggled to find the matches in the half light of the evening, but soon had them in my grasp, inhaling the soft sulphurous smell as the flare softly lit up the interior. I lit the many candles, and with each movement of the match, the photograph of Ross became clearer, emerging from the darkness, until he was there, smiling at me with his familiar, cheerful face.

I pulled up the old chair, placing my mug of hot chocolate among the candles where it steamed comfortingly. Gazing up at my brother, the tears came again for a while as I remembered all we had lost. Pulling myself together, I drew the chair closer to the photo.

"You'll never guess where I've been tonight, Ross," I began. "Nope, not the Train yard. Not even McDonald's. I've been back to St Peter's, and it was…"

The door behind me opened quietly. So much for our Jilly not disturbing me, I thought hotly, looking back to see who was spoiling my moment. Then with a smile I saw Flora's head and right arm, waving through the entrance at me. What on earth… I stood up and moved to the door. The dummy came fully into the shed, wearing Jilly's best new leather jacket and smelling of some expensive perfume which I recognized as Mam's. Outside, struggling to hold her up, was our Jilly.

"I knew you wouldn't want me in here with you, Will," she told me quietly, "but this one insisted you had some female company. There you go." And she handed Flora over and shut the door gently, moving back up the garden in the evening mist. I smiled to myself and took Flora to sit beside me in front of Ross's photo.

"Right, bro – where was I?" I asked him. "Oh yes, St Peter's," I sniffed. "And by the way, this is Flora. Flora, this is Ross, my big brother."

***

A couple of hours later I was lying on my bed, doing what most teenage boys are really good at: *absolutely nothing*. I really did feel a bit better having talked to Ross, and Flora proved to be the perfect companion – quiet, attentive and beautiful. She didn't make any wisecracks, ask stupid questions or run out to see if her eyelashes were still on. There was no checking her mobile, biting her nails, or trying to take a selfie. She just listened to me droning on to our Ross and didn't once judge me.

I told him how much we all missed him, how Mam and Jilly were starting to pull themselves together again, but that they both still had their 'crying-in-the-shower' moments. I explained that Dad was being the strong silent type for the rest of us, and from somewhere inside my head I got this notion that I should get Dad to do exactly what I was doing: coming into the shed to off-load to Ross. To clear the air, clear my head and my heart.

Jilly later said that Mam had asked where I was, and my sister had told her I'd 'gone to Confession'. I mean, really? Me, go to Confession in St Peter's? Durr... but, thinking about it, wasn't that what I *was* doing, only here in the shed, instead of in a church, and with only Ross listening, plus Flora, not Fr Raff.

Eventually, Flora and I had made our way back into the house and up the stairs. I could hear my parents in the living room, complaining about something happening on Masterchef, but bat-ears Mam heard me.

"Will? Is that you? Are you ok?"

"Fine, Mam, now," I replied.

"Have you got your mates with you?" she asked, ever suspicious and rather accusingly, I thought.

"Just the one beautiful girl, Mam, but don't worry: she's quite safe with me. In my bedroom." I smiled, bumping Flora up the stairs with me. My dad gave a rare, muffled chuckle in the living room beside her, and I swear I heard him mutter, "Atta boy, Will," at which point he would have received a dig from my mam. Sitting Flora rather sedately on the chair in front of my desk, I cleared away my Maths homework, completed as well, but probably completely wrong, checked on Nigel underneath my bed, and wondered how Keith was enjoying being in church with the lads. I had no real concerns about Keith: I knew he was in safe hands with Rob and Gaz. And they were in safe hands with Raff. I mean, you wouldn't take your chances on a guy like that – he was built like a Rugby Full Back.

I put my headphones on to listen to some music, but it simply irritated me, so I pulled them back off again. I picked up a magazine from the bedside cabinet, but the words refused to sink into my brain. None of it made any sense, so I dropped it on the floor. That's how Gaz must feel most of the time, I smiled to myself. Poor Gaz – gormless and gawky, but always had my back. My friends had proved to be my lifeline since we lost Ross. They knew how to pick me up when I was down, could tell without asking how I was feeling, and were always ready with a joke or a dead leg to wake me up and bring me back to earth when I was in danger of going under.

I wondered about Jimmy Jesus. We really had to get our act together and find the old guy, but where to start? I hoped Jimmy was in a safe place, away from prying eyes, and had a full belly and a warm blanket. I know he was used to his life, but the old chap wasn't getting any younger, and the recent attack on him could so easily happen again. I planned on getting together with the lads, possibly with Mr Angus as well, to see if he could offer any suggestions. At least that way, the school would know we were serious about helping Jimmy and weren't just messing about like we normally did.

I think I dozed off at one point, dreaming of seeing Jimmy wearing a smart suit and a set of dentures which would make Shergar proud, when I heard the unmistakable sound of stones hitting my bedroom window. When the third pebble took on the size of a half brick, I leapt from my bed to open the window before it smashed to bits. Below me I could make out three figures, standing on Mam's daffodils. The lads were back.

"Oy, watch it you three," I told them in hushed tones. "Make your way down to the shed and I'll join you out there. Mam won't be very happy to know you've turned up this late."

I got two thumbs up and an alabaster wave from Keith as the three of them hobbled down towards the back of the garden. Smiling at the sight of them, I put my Sponge Bob slippers on, quietly crept down the stairs, through the kitchen, and made my way to join them.

They had lit some of the candles by the time I joined them, and although the lighting was quite dim, it made for a cosy scene. As I wandered through the door, I noticed Keith propped up at the back against the window, his cap pulled down over his face, leaning drunkenly to one side. Rob and Gaz were standing nervously with their backs to the picture of Ross, and in the candlelight, I couldn't quite make out the expression on their faces. Knowing them as well as I did, however, I knew straight away that something was up. I could feel the nerves emanating from them. I could almost smell it – like when you lift the lid on a pan of sprouts boiling away in your kitchen: you just know this is going to taste bad.

Gaz was bouncing from one foot to the other, twisting his hands in front of him. Rob seemed calmer, but the way his shoulders drooped and he looked up at me through his fringe worried me.

"What?" I demanded. "What's happened? Come on, you two. I know something's up. Spill."

"Ok," he began, glancing first at Gaz, then over towards Keith, "it could be worse, mate," he told me, pushing a hand through his hair and pulling a bit of a face. Now I was getting worried. What had they done, these three? I mean, just how much trouble could you get up to inside a Catholic Church? Gaz sniffed and rubbed his nose on his sleeve.

"Oh no, he hasn't had his hand in the collection basket, has he?" I gestured towards Gaz but spoke to Rob. Rob shook his head, and almost smiled. Gaz's head snapped up and he attempted to look shocked, but it didn't quite work. I sighed.

"Has he set the place alight? I know he used to light all the candles in the church when we were in year two," I reminded them both. "And his hair, once."

"No, nothing like that, Will," Rob replied. "His pyromaniac days are well and truly over."

"It's because we saw Jimmy, Will. We were only trying to catch Jimmy," Gaz said, rubbing his hair and sniffing in Keith's direction again.

"Well, it was the flamin' bus driver's fault really," Rob told Gaz, raising his eyebrows at him in warning. I stared from one to the other, trying to make sense of what had happened.

"Ok," I told them firmly, sitting down near Ross's photo in front of the candles. "Let's start at the beginning, shall we? I left you three, in St Peter's, with Fr O'Rafferty. I went home. What happened next?"

Rob sat down beside me on an old stool. Gaz moved to stand near the window, beside Keith. I noticed he took hold of Keith's hand, but because it was Gaz, it didn't seem odd at all. He can be quite touchy-feely can our Gaz. In the flickering half-light of the shed, he looked a bit like an Old Masters oil painting, all dramatic and moody.

"So…" began Rob. "We spoke to Raff about the fashion show in a few weeks, and he seemed really keen to have the dummies involved, as well as us." He spoke quietly, occasionally glancing towards Gaz and Keith.

"But we're going to be the stars of the show," Gaz interjected, "not the dummies. Well, us and Fiona Bridges…" and he bit the nail of his thumb then, looking nervous. I raised my eyebrows at him, then at Rob. What, Fiona Bridges, on stage, with us and the dummies? Why were these two numpties not leaping about in delight? I didn't get it.

What were they not telling me? Rob narrowed his eyes at Gaz and continued his story.

"We told Raff we'd come back later in the week, after we'd told you all about it. We didn't want you to feel left out of it you see, Will."

I shrugged at him. "Right. And...?"

"We decided we'd get the bus home, because we were dying to tell you that Fiona, *and her friends*, are going to be in the fashion show with us, you see." My mate looked up, eyes blazing at that point. I knew there was more than this though, so I couldn't feel the sense of excitement I should have been feeling, only a sense of dread.

"Go on," I commanded.

"The bus came and we got on it. The driver was a bit of a git, mind," Rob told me.

"A bit?" Gaz jumped in. "He was a right old bas..." Rob cut him off.

"We only had enough money for our bus fares you see, Will. But yeah, Gaz is right. He was a tightfisted old skinflint. He wanted to charge us full adult fare for Keith!"

"Well, we weren't having that," Gaz said, getting all angry and steamed up. "I mean, our Keith..." and he patted the dummy on the head, gently.

"So, we argued the toss with the driver," Rob explained. "Then some of the old dears on the bus were getting angry cos they thought they'd be late for their Bingo session."

"I was going to get off and told the driver I'd report him to the bus company," Gaz informed me, eyes all animated with anger.

"But..." Rob put in. "One old bloke at the back of the bus thought Keith looked like his grandson, so he gave us the bus fare for him."

I had been turning my head from one to the other as they told their tale, and now I was feeling quite dizzy. I sat back and rubbed my hands over my face.

"So, you three caused a bit of a ruck on the bus," I began, looking at my mates.

"Aye, the number twenty-seven," added Gaz, gravely, as if that made any difference.

"You held it up and caused a scene for a few minutes, angering all the passengers." I was trying to picture it in my befuddled head.

"Some of them thought it was better than EastEnders." Gaz smiled at the memory of the fat old dear on the front seat who had chuckled all the way through the altercation with the bus driver.

"Well, yeah," Rob replied, but continued. "So, when us three were finally on our way back to yours, Will, we were just going over the bridge when Gaz leapt out of his seat, and started shouting."

At this point Gaz began his re-enactment, leaping to his feet from his position next to Keith, arms pointing wildly to the front, eyes staring like a madman.

"Jesus! Look, Rob, he's over there!"

Rob held up a hand to calm him down a bit. "Ok, Gaz. I'll take it from here. Well, Will, some of the oldies on the bus thought he was having hallucinations. They thought our Gaz might have been a visionary," he smiled.

"More likely they thought he was off his head," I smiled back, picturing Gaz on the bus, passengers watching him, mouths agape.

"But no, he'd spotted Jimmy, going down the steps near the bridge, towards the docks…"

I sat there, open-mouthed at this tale. Why did these three have all the fun? And we had nearly lost Keith in the process!

"Whoa, lads. That's pretty epic," I told them, as Gaz moved to bring Keith into the light from his position near the window. "Well, you might have lost Jimmy again but at least you didn't lose Keith. Well done, guys," I said. Then my face fell.

Rob and Gaz took off Keith's hat and I saw him properly for the first time since I had left him in their care inside St Peter's. His face was all bashed in on one side, there was a gaping hole in his cheek, and he had only one arm. Jilly's blue coat was ripped to bits, and one whole sleeve was missing.

"Sorry, Will," Rob told me, crestfallen, his head hanging.

"We only lost a bit of Keith," Gaz told me, nervously. "The rest of him is fine."

The shed door flew open, and we four jumped back, expecting an angry parent, a manager from the bus company, or a Police Officer at least. It was worse than that. It was our Jilly, and one look at her pink nightie, dressing gown flapping in the breeze, bare feet and absolutely flaming face told us we were in deep doo-doo. She nearly took the door off its hinges as she stormed into the shed to join us, mobile phone in hand, eyes aflame.

"*Right,*" she hissed, trying to remain both quiet and in control, and failing miserably. "*I want some answers from you morons.*"

Beside me, Gaz gulped and whimpered. I heard Rob swallow loudly and watched fascinated as his Adam's apple bobbed up and down with nerves and fear. And truly, Jilly was a fearsome sight. Where was the kind, supportive and sweet girl from only a short time ago? In front of us now was this raging she-monster, eyes bulging, hair on end and mobile phone held out in a fist clenched as tight as her teeth were. She was visibly shaking.

"Jilly, what on earth…" I began, as she came towards us, menacingly, into the shed.

Rob put both hands up, in self-defence I thought, and began to stammer.

"Now Jilly, I'm sure it looks worse than it really is…" he began, but she flew at him, shoving him down onto the stool. Next, she slammed me down onto the chair and thrust her mobile into my hands.

"This is what your stupid friends have been up to," she told me, lighting up her mobile, and waving a Facebook page in my face.

Rob groaned, as Gaz began to mutter, "Facebook? We don't do Facebook, Jilly, that's only for the oldies…" but one look from her blazing eyes shut him up instantly.

Glancing at my mates, I took the phone from her and pressed play on the video. It was obviously filmed from the back seat of the bus. The back of people's heads were obvious, as was the startling image of Gaz standing in the aisle. It'll be easier to describe it like this:

Gaz: Jesus! Look Rob, he's over there!

Rob: (standing up to join him near the front doors) No, it can't be him. Is it?

Gaz: It's him, for defo. Driver, stop the bus!

Driver: Sit down, you bloody idiots. Whoever it is, it's NOT Jesus! Are you two on something?

Gaz: No, it really is him. We've been after him for ages. Please, Mister, stop the bus before we lose him again.

Driver: (angry, shaking his head) Nee chance. We're still on the bridge. This isn't a designated bus stop. Bloody kids…

Woman 1: Don't even think about it you. (Pointing to driver) I want to get home for me tea.

Woman 2: And I'm already late for Bingo. Keep going or I'll report you to the bus company.

Man 1: Let the lads off the bus, man – then we can all get some peace and get to where we're going.

Woman 3: I haven't had this much fun since VE day… Go on, son. You stick to your guns.

Drunk at the back: I saw Henry the Eighth in the Queen's Head the other night, but Jesus takes some beating, mind.

Drunken mate beside him: Doesn't he play for Man Utd or summat?

Drunk: Who? Henry the Eighth?

Drunk Mate: Idiot – he died yonks ago. I mean Jesus.

Gaz: (to driver) Right, if you don't do something about it, I will. (Leans forward and presses a large red button near the door which stops the bus in its tracks. The doors open with a hiss. Car horns are heard from outside, swear words from inside. The driver leaps out of his seat and grabs Rob by his jacket. He forces Rob violently off the bus onto the bridge.)

Rob: Ow, get off me. I want me mates an' all, mind!

(Gaz grabs Keith and struggles to get the dummy out of the open bus doors. Gaz jumps down onto the road, leaving Keith wedged on the steps of the bus.)

Woman 2: Great – I've missed the first full line now, and all because a couple of mangy teenagers have found God on Monkwearmouth Bridge. Why can't you go back to hanging around on street corners, breaking bottles, eh?

Driver: Stupid sods! Bugger off. I'm calling the police. You're holding up all the traffic. Now, sod off!

(He gets back into his seat, presses a button to close the doors and begins to drive off. A scream can be heard from outside on the road. Rob and Gaz can briefly be seen jumping up and down, waving their arms and attempting to hold up Keith. From outside on the bridge, Rob makes a dive at the door of the bus, where inside, an arm, wearing a tattered blue sleeve, slowly drops to the floor. Man 1 gets up, holds up the arm and waves it at all the passengers. Cheering breaks out. The camera is pointed then out of the back window of the bus where Rob, Gaz and Keith are desperately dodging traffic as it begins to make its way over the bridge. Hoots of car horns, and the sounds of hoots of laughter from inside the bus.)

I shook my head, handed the phone back to my sister and looked at Gaz and Rob. They had gone very quiet, eyes shiftily looking about the shed in Gaz's case, as if searching for an exit; Rob's hands were covering his face.

"Any comments or observations?" I asked, sarcastically. All was quiet for a minute, except for the sound of the candles hissing quietly and Jilly breathing heavily in anger.

"Jilly," Gaz began, staring at her earnestly. "You don't half look sexy in that nightie."

Chapter 15

We were the talk of the town again after that, well, I say the town, what I really mean is the saddos in school, Rob's footy team and the chip shop on the corner. Everyone had heard about our antics on the bus. One of the girls from our Citizenship class decided to raise some funds through Facebook to repair Keith – "alms" though, she called it, ha ha. We laughed it off at first, until Rob pointed out that any funds raised could go towards the rescue of Jimmy, and our Jilly's new blue coat.

In the shed, she'd had to be held back off Gaz, foaming at the mouth, when he said he'd seen one very similar in the Oxfam shop, and that even though the hem was hanging down, and one pocket was bigger than the other, she could soon put that right, a talented girl like her.

We were all grounded – of course. That goes without saying, but really, I mean, come on: none of what happened that night was my fault, was it? It was those two numpties on the bus, with Keith. Poor Keith! He was a mess. We couldn't put him on the catwalk now, could we? We were a man down. We all felt really bad about him. Rob said he kept having a recurring dream where Keith's face and head got mashed by a steamroller or some other heavy vehicle, and I swear my mate developed a twitch shortly after. Gaz just seemed oblivious: a bit dim and withdrawn perhaps, but, hey, it's Gaz. What's new?

Jilly went stratospheric, as only Jilly can. She wailed; she screamed; she slapped me (me??); she slammed doors; she stormed around the house like a whirling dervish until I retreated to my room to get some peace, my sanctuary, although my Xbox and PlayStation had been confiscated for a fortnight. I had promised to try to get a paper round, a car cleaning round, mug a Bingo-winner or something, so I could begin to pay her back for the damage to her coat. And all this, just when the sort of sister I always dreamed about having had been starting to emerge, like a chrysalis before me, looking after her only baby bro. Oh well. Back to the drawing board, eh?

We three saw each other in school, of course, but it wasn't quite the same when we couldn't arrange to meet up after Neighbours and go for a mooch about together with Flora, or Nige. I knew the dummies were feeling a bit bored and neglected too. They were still in my room, Nige stuffed in the wardrobe, legless, and Flora sat at my desk, demure and silent, like a redundant secretary. I had thought about stashing Nigel's legs in Jilly's bed, feet sticking out the bottom of her duvet, and his hands reaching up behind her pillows, but she'd been through enough trauma already and I didn't fancy wearing my bits as earrings…

We plotted and schemed as best we could through social media and texting each other, but we had to be careful. No information could be filtered back to the flapping lugs of Mick and Bernice. We also didn't want the school or Mr Angus to know that we hadn't even made personal contact with Jimmy yet, let alone set up an action plan, or spoken to any Authority figures about the old guy and the rosy future we were going to supply him with. I was really beginning to feel out of my depth, to be honest.

At first, it had seemed like a brilliant idea, a chance to really prove ourselves, to do something worthwhile and get some well-earned glory. In reality, however, it was becoming a nightmare. I mean, there were so many questions we three simply hadn't thought of, like where to *find* the old guy first. Jimmy was like The Scarlet Pimpernel; now you see him, now you don't. We had no idea about where we could 'house' him once we did manage to track him down. Gaz suggested just knocking on the door of that Happy Valley Retirement Home and running away, leaving Jimmy sort of slumped up against the door-bell. We pointed out to Gaz that these places charge a fortune, they don't just let any old bloke in, and certainly not one who didn't have a penny to his name, had some very peculiar habits and smelled like the bottom of a fish barrel.

Honestly, it was all flying round inside my head like a mini tornado and was keeping me awake at night. Flamin' Rob and his clever ideas, eh? Gaz, on the other hand, simply didn't have the mental capacity to move on from our running feud with Big Bird and her henchman, Mad Mick. They'd been spotted on a few occasions, holding hands and sort of slurping over each other's faces. Yuk! Totally sick making, that image. If Gaz spotted them, he usually threw something at them before legging it. Nothing more dangerous than a pinecone, a bit of stick, or on one occasion, a plant pot full of dead daffs. They had returned his half-hearted attempts to catch their attention with bellowed abuse, fists in his direction and a swift kick up the backside by Bernice when she spotted Gaz coming out of the barbers with his dad.

Rob, of course, being the clever one of us three, spent his grounded time trying to come up with a plan. He asked questions about Jimmy to anyone who would listen – not many, it seemed. He wandered around the town centre on his own, well, walking next door's dog as part of his punishment; he said it was punishment because it was a Pug, and was Pug-ugly and fat. But all the while he was out with Stanley, he kept his eyes and ears open, looking for Jimmy. The old fella was elusive, to say the least. People either threw money in Jimmy's direction, had a mind-numbing chat with him as they handed over a cup of tea, or just gave him a friendly wave and kept their distance to avoid the smell. And the fleas, as we knew to our cost.

Eventually our two-week purgatory was up, and we were allowed to meet up once again, but with certain restrictions. We were not allowed near the Railyard. Tut. We had to avoid the town centre and any buses after about six pm at night. Tut. And we had to avoid all contact with Jilly and Steve, or risk getting our heads knocked off by them both. We decided to meet up in our shed.

I took Keith, because I felt bad about his injury and didn't want him to feel socially isolated and inadequate due to a facial disfigurement. You read about these things, don't you? Well, I do anyway. It was in Jilly's Girl Talk magazine the other week. A teenage boy with cross eyes and acne had tried to jump off a bridge but had been prevented from doing it by an attractive girl on her way to the dentist. It was all a bit improbable, but it had a happy ending because her mam turned out to be a surgeon and she pointed the lad in the direction of the people who could help him. If only he found his way, of course, his vision being what it was... But hey, it left a lasting impression on me, and I didn't want Keith's future chances of happiness, and his modelling career, left in tatters. Unlike his face.

I stood him near the window so he could keep his remaining eye open for the lads arriving while I had a chat with Ross.

Lighting the little candles, even though it was quite a sunny evening, I glanced up at the picture of my brother. He was smiling back at me, his face sort of shining from behind the lectern, and it felt like he was giving me his most encouraging smile. Taking a duster from the drawer of the old desk, I gently wiped the whole photograph, frame and all, because some of the sheen had been covered by a year or more of dust. I polished up the gilt frame, but when it came to Ross's face, I slowed down and was gentle. I had a sudden flash of my mam tenderly wiping his mouth with a tea towel after he had been eating a chocolate ice cream when he was about 11 and I would have been about five. Ross had squirmed and laughed, trying to get away from her, but eventually given in to a big kiss on the cheek as he cheerily left the house.

Sitting on the stool in front of him, I sighed and asked my brother, "Come on, Ross. I need a hand here, you know. I'm a bit lost about what to do about this Jimmy thing. It seemed like such a good idea at first."

Ross smiled brightly back at me in the flickering candlelight. I could hear him, in my head, and in my heart. My brother's voice came clearly back to me.

"You can't really back out now, Will. This project has some merit, you know. You just need to take your time and assess the situation fully."

"It wasn't my idea," I told him. "It was Rob. Trust him to come up with something like this. And now we're a bit lost about what to do next. I'd tell him to forget all about it, but I don't want to let my mates down, do I?"

Ross's smile seemed to move in the candlelight, as if he were pondering my statement. Did my brother think I was chickening out? Was *I* thinking of chickening out? I glanced up as the door squeaked open and Gaz appeared, carefully popping his head into the shed to check the coast was clear before entering. I gestured him in.

As Gaz hesitated near Keith, inspecting his damaged face with a frown, I heard Ross's reply quite clearly.

"If Rob came up with this idea, he'll find a way to sort it. You watch, Will. He's a bright lad is your mate. Have some faith in him."

"How's he doing?" I heard a voice behind me. Gaz, gesturing to the photo of Ross, being all quiet and reverent-like. I smiled back at my friend.

"He's ok, Gaz," I told him.

"Do you think he's happy?" Gaz asked, staring at the picture. I raised my eyebrows at Gaz. What a thing to ask. I'd never thought about Ross's "happiness", just our sadness at losing him the way we did. Maybe because I always pictured Ross smiling, like his photograph, or playing his guitar, or laughing in a bar with his student mates, I told Gaz, "Yes, mate, I believe he is happy now."

"Oh good," Gaz said, smiling gently and reaching out to stroke the photo. He stood very quietly in front of it, staring at the image of my big brother. Gaz has a big brother, and a little one as well, but they don't really get on, not like I did with Ross. My friend gave a sigh which seemed to come up from his boots.

"You know, Will, of all the people in the world, your Ross was the last one we thought would have died like that," he told me solemnly. I moved to stand beside him. He glanced up at me quickly. "Soz, mate. Is it ok for me to say that?"

Giving him a pat on the back, I gulped and nodded my head. Gaz took that as permission to carry on.

"If it had been *my* elder brother, it wouldn't have been such a shock," he told me. "Because he's done some pretty stupid and dangerous things in his time. But not your Ross. He was the best," he added. "I mean, *drugs*? He didn't even smoke fags, let alone take something as dodgy as the stuff that killed him."

I exhaled a shaky breath and shook my head in agreement. "I know, mate. What was he thinking of? We knew he was always up for a laugh, but *that* …"

I fought to keep a flashback of that nightmare night out of my head. I could feel it snaking its way towards me, like a dragon, spitting at me and breathing fire. I think I caught my breath because suddenly Gaz put an arm around my shoulders, hugging me tight.

"He was definitely spiked, Will," Gaz asserted. "Definitely. Your Ross would never knowingly take something that dangerous. He wouldn't put the family through that much stress."

I gulped and nodded, looking into the face of my brother, that innocent, handsome, intelligent face I missed so much. Together we stepped back from the photo, like we'd seen the priest doing on the altar in church – quietly, reverently, with respect.

"Rob will be here in a minute. His match ran into extra time," Gaz explained in a more cheerful voice.

The moment was gone.

I sighed and grinned at my mate. "Well of course it did. And how many has he scored this time?"

"Only two. But someone got a late goal in and they were drawing, last I heard."

I went to the cupboard and took out two cans of fizzy pop, telling Gaz as I did so, "You know, Gaz, we must make a decision about this Citizenship project with Jimmy. We're going nowhere fast with this and I'm really worried."

As Gaz opened the can with a clack, he nodded, took a big drink and eyed me over the top of it.

"Me an' all, Will," he replied. "I think it's going to be a disaster. I think someone's going to end up in big trouble." He took a slurp of his drink and wiped his mouth on his sleeve, looking at me seriously.

"I know, mate," I told him, "I feel it in my water. And if anything is going to go wrong, it'll be us three that gets into trouble. And it's not as if we always set out to make a mess of things. It just… *happens*."

Gaz gazed out of the shed window, speaking quietly as he did so.

"If it was just you and me, you know, Will, I'd say it was guaranteed to fail." I gave him a wry smile. "But because it was Rob's idea we might just make something of it, because he doesn't usually get stuff spectacularly wrong, like us two."

I was grudgingly agreeing with Gaz when the door squeaked open and in bounced the man himself, Rob. He was sort of glowing with health and pride. He looked freshly scrubbed and windswept, happy to see us, and obviously with a tale to tell.

"Alright, lads?" he asked, as I handed him a can. His mood was catching, and just having him beside us in the close confines of the shed, I could feel my anxiety about Jimmy lifting a little, as though a dark cloud was drifting away from me.

"I take it you won then?" I asked him. "What was the final score?"

"Three, two, to us," he told us, grinning. "And guess who scored the last goal?"

Gaz jumped up from his seat. "NO way man!" He declared, clapping Rob on the back. "You scored a hat trick?"

I was amazed. I knew our mate was good on the pitch – we'd spent hours in the rain and cold cheering him on from the sidelines. No wonder the teachers all loved Rob; and every girl from year nine upwards come to think of it. Such a star, this lad.

"You got all the goals in the match?" I asked, incredulously, pride racing through me like a warm wave. Wow.

"We have to celebrate, lads," I told them.

"Later," Rob replied, gratefully downing his can. "I have an idea about where we might find Jimmy," he told us, brimming with excitement. I felt both deflated and curious all at the same time. Bang goes my chance to get us out of this situation, I thought. Rob's on the game again.

We sat down wherever we could, but not before Rob had gone over to Keith and given him a conciliatory high five on his one remaining hand, straightening his cap and jacket, and standing him up safely. We squatted together in the dim light of the shed, leaning in towards each other expectantly. From his photo, even Ross seemed fully engaged with the scene before him.

"So, you know when we got thrown off the bus on the bridge?" Rob began. "Where was Jimmy going?" He raised his eyebrows at Gaz.

Gaz's face clouded in thought. He looked like he was brewing something nasty, but whenever Gaz concentrates, his face does that. He sat up straighter, obviously thinking carefully.

"Er, down the steps, underneath the bridge…" he began. I looked at the two of them, wondering where this was going.

"And?" I asked, shaking my head at the two of them.

Rob continued eagerly. "And… that side of the bridge leads to one of the least favourite riverside walks in the town, and the old fish quay, doesn't it?"

I sat back and thought about the place, picturing the old boats, the sheds, the fishy-smelling equipment lying forlornly around on the waterside.

"But, nobody really goes down there, do they?" Gaz asked. "Only a few fishermen and some old guys who have boats moored down there. It's all a bit whiffy, actually. In fact, it stinks."

Rob sat bolt upright in triumph, raising his can, as if in a toast.

"And so does Jimmy, doesn't he?"

Gaz and I exchanged puzzled glances.

"Jimmy stinks of fish!" Rob declared. "And nobody goes down there. That's where we'll find our man, lads. Think about it. It's perfect for him!"

I could feel the smile beginning to spread over my face, warming to Rob's enthusiasm. Glancing at the picture of Ross, I raised my can to him, then chinked cans with my mates.

"So, what are we waiting for, boys?" I asked them brightly.

Chapter 16

Having been grounded for two weeks after damaging Jilly's coat, Keith, and for (allegedly) causing chaos on a bus, we three were giddy with excitement to be back out again. It felt like we had been released from prison. We had been told in no uncertain terms to stay away from buses, from trying to wind up Big Bird and Mick – as if we would – and not to hang around the city centre while we were looking for Jimmy.

The Dummies had to stay home too, which we felt was unfair. I mean, Flora was completely innocent in anything that had already gone on. She sat around in my bedroom looking bored and listless. In fact, as Rob pointed out, she was beginning to gather dust. I was quite horrified at that. Nige was starting to look like a real old bloke, his pale grey eyes stared wistfully at me from the deeper recesses of my wardrobe. His legs were still under my bed, his arms were now in a drawer. I had hung them on a piece of string over the banister, just for a laugh, like you do, but my dad had walked into them at three o'clock in the morning, coming from a sly cig at the back door, and in the dark he thought someone had broken into the house and was having a go at him. He really wasn't interested in the fact that the prank had been aimed at Jilly coming in late from a nightclub. In his panic, Dad had blundered about and punched a hole in the wall. Later he pointed out that if it *had* been Jilly who had walked into Nigel's arms, she would have punched a hole in my head, so all in all, it was better it was my dad who fell for Nigel's charms. Or should that be arms...?

As the weather was warming up nicely, me and Gaz took the dummies outside and sat Flora and Nigel together on the picnic bench near the shed. To gain a few more brownie points, we had told Mam that we'd do a spring clean of the shed and the garden furniture before the real summer weather came. In actual fact, we just wanted to make the dummies feel a bit better. They had been grounded for even longer than us lads had, and to my knowledge, neither of those two had been up to anything wrong.

I brushed Flora's wig, Gaz touched up Nigel's ash-grey hair with a mascara wand which appeared magically from his pocket, and we sat them opposite each other at the bench outside in the sun. I swear that they instantly looked brighter. Gaz insisted on placing a can of drink from the shed in front of them, but I stopped him from raiding the cupboards for biscuits on a posh plate. Well, he *said* they were for the dummies, but I had my suspicions.

Rob was coming along a bit later, so Gaz and I went into the shed to have a word with Keith. We hadn't told the other two dummies that their friend was so badly disfigured. We were going to hang on until Rob arrived so that we could tell them together. We knew it would be a shock to them, and Gaz wanted them to experience a little bit of normality by sitting together in the sun before we gave them a shock.

Poor Keith. He was still standing in the corner of the shed where we'd left him, leaning forlornly into a corner with his face to the wall. From the back he still looked like the dapper, handsome chap we knew him to be. Front on was a different matter though. I sighed, feeling heartily sorry for him.

"Can't you get make-up for him?" asked Gaz, peering up at Keith's battered face.

"I don't think a slap of foundation is going to do it, mate," I told him, turning Keith round to the light and wiping a cobweb from his head.

"I meant that heavy-duty stuff that burns victims use," Gaz told me.

I gazed at Keith, trying to work out what would be best for him. There was no way he'd be able to join the rest of us on the catwalk for St Peter's fashion show in his current state.

"Maybe a mask?" I suggested. "Like the ones you wear in Drama."

"Polyfilla might do it," Gaz replied, after a moment, his eyebrows raised questioningly to me. I had a vision of Gaz with a bucket of wet cement and a trowel in his hand as he loomed over the lovely Keith and shuddered. Just then, a can rolled over from the picnic table outside, and I thought I heard the unmistakable click of the garden gate.

Popping my head out of the shed door, I quickly took in the scene in front of me, and equally quickly looked back at my mate beside me.

"What?" Gaz asked.

My mouth opened and closed a couple of times, I shook my head and dragged Gaz's head out of the door, pointing to the bench.

"*What?*" Again, he demanded.

"Look at Nigel and Flora!" I told him. He looked, then looked again more closely.

"Ahh." He smiled. "They're holding hands."

I took another quick look, shaking my head in disbelief. "Yeah, they are," I told him, "but we left them sitting opposite each other, didn't we? Not side by side like that."

Now it was Gaz's turn to look puzzled. "Er, did we? I didn't take that much notice," he told me. Looking at his face, now I wasn't sure myself.

"Anyway, back to Keith. Where are we going to find another arm for him, even if we can fix his face?"

Gaz pondered for a moment, then his face lit up. "Got it," he began. I looked at him expectantly. "He can just borrow one off Nige."

I sighed. Where was Rob when I needed him most?

"Look, mate," I pointed out, "Nigel needs both of his arms for himself, don't you think?"

Gaz had the grace to blush a bit, but straightening Keith up inside the shed, he told me, quite solemnly and firmly, "Well personally I think he still should be in the fashion show. It's all about diversity and inclusivity these days, you know. *And,*" he continued, "there might be someone in the audience with only one arm. So, thought of that had we?"

I took another glance into the garden to see if there was any sign of Rob, racing to my rescue. Once again, I took hold of Gaz's arm and drew him outside towards the dummies. Now, Flora had her head on Nigel's shoulder and was looking quite smug about it!

"What the…" I began.

Gaz just laughed. "Must be the wind made her topple over." He grinned as we approached our two friends outside in the still evening air.

When we reached them, I sat Flora up into a more comfortable position, straightening her skirt to keep her decent. She certainly had a glint in her eye I wasn't sure I'd seen before, little minx. Gaz's laughter made me glance up at him. His shoulders were shaking, his eyes gleaming as he giggled with delight.

"What now?" I asked him, confused.

Gaz turned Nigel's head to face me and Flora; there was a lipstick mark on his right cheek, a bright red kiss.

"What the…" I began, touching the dummy's cool porcelain cheek where, indeed, the lipstick mark slipped beneath my fingers. It was fresh lipstick!

Quickly I searched Flora's face. Where she had previously been pale and interesting, now she was wearing bright red lippy. Gaz had spotted it on her mouth too and was laughing uproariously.

"Flora – you tart!" he told her. "Are you trying to snog our Nigel? He's getting on a bit, you know, girl."

"Did you do this, Gaz?" I asked him, but, really, I knew he hadn't had time. He'd been in the shed with me and Keith. He looked shocked at that.

"Me? No! I don't go round kissing old blokes, do I? It was her," he stated, pointing at Flora. Honestly, I half expected to see her blushing, but she sat there, as cool as a cucumber.

My head was in a spin. Glancing round the garden, I could see that Rob wasn't hiding somewhere behind a bush or a bin, ready to jump out with a "ta dah!". Two doors down, old Mr Seymour was putting something in his bins, but he'd just had a new hip, so there was no way he could have cleared two gardens and got back into his own in the time it took for him to apply the lipstick and us to spot it.

"Right, Gaz," I announced. "Empty your pockets." He gave me a surprised shrug.

"Me? What for?" he asked, clearly affronted.

"A bright red lipstick for a start." I told him, starting to frisk him down, which set him off giggling like a two-year-old again. He jumped back, stumbled and grabbed out for me, but I had my hands down his jumper, so the two of us ended up rolling around on the grass, slapping at each other's hands and generally getting sillier and sweatier by the minute, until a pair of trainers appeared by our heads and a voice coughed, ostentatiously.

"Am I interrupting something here, ladies? I can always go away and come back when you two have, you know... finished?"

We lay on our backs in the grass, shielding our eyes against the evening sun.

"Rob!" we exclaimed, getting up to meet our mate. He was back from his match, an important one, we knew, and we were anxious to hear how he'd got on.

Gaz and I were expecting our usual bright and bouncy mate, pumped up with exercise and success, but for once Rob looked quite downcast. His shoulders were slumped and his eyes flashed with anger, or despair.

"Mate?" I asked him, guiding him to sit down on the bench opposite Flora and Nige. "Didn't you win?" I asked him quietly. "Did you not score this time?"

Gaz and I stood behind the two dummies, looking carefully at our friend, our sporting superhero.

Rob put his face into his hands, rubbing his eyes for a minute before looking up with a bleak expression to tell us, "Oh, I scored alright. A bloody own goal."

We glanced at each other, shocked. I gently moved Flora out of the way, onto the grass, so I could sit opposite Rob. I couldn't believe our Rob could do that. Gaz was so shocked he simply grabbed Nige by the lapels and flung him to the ground, before leaping into the seat the dummy had just been unceremoniously dumped from.

"Come on, Rob," he told him gently. "Tell us everything. This was your big chance, wasn't it?"

Rob stared at us both, then glanced at the dummies on the ground, but barely registered their presence. He looked away, over the trees, down the street, tears shining in his eyes.

"We were doing great, lads, to begin with," he began. "There was a good crowd of supporters and Middleton had brought loads of their own because it was the semi-final. I was on good form to begin with, but then some of their supporters seemed to be getting at me, and only me." He paused, during which time Gaz and I shook our heads in disbelief. Rob is a brilliant player, very popular, always on hand to set up a goal, or get one for himself. Why would anyone on the sidelines have a go at him? It didn't make sense.

"Are you sure it was you they were having a go at?" Gaz asked gently.

"Hell, yeah," Rob told us. "Every time I got near the ball. Boos, hisses, catcalls, laughter if I made the smallest mistake, and of course I started to, because they were putting me off."

I knew this was a big game, and that some banter always occurred, but this was obviously bigger and more threatening to have affected

Rob like this.

"Some of the lads cottoned on and the Ref had a word with the supporters, but they only moved to the other side of the pitch and continued from over there," Rob told us. "And I know I can normally ignore any of the rubbish they shout, but this time it got to me." His voice was quiet, but he was starting to get quite red in the face with anger and frustration.

"I made the mistake of gobbing off back at them," he told us bleakly, "and of course that just made it worse. I got into trouble off the Ref, then when I headed in an own goal, I was taken off."

Rob – taken off the pitch! *An own goal?* We couldn't believe it. It was all quite unthinkable. We sat up straight and gazed at him, shocked.

"Who was it?" Gaz asked in a cold voice.

Rob sat up straight, fiddling with one of the cans on the table, before telling us bleakly, "Well, guess who? Big Bird and some of her coven."

We were thunderstruck. Big Bird? At a match? We stared at Rob's pinched face with eyes like saucers.

Gazing back at us, he told us, "Her cousin was playing for Middleton, the opposition. When she saw me on the pitch, she was determined to put me off. And stupidly, I played right into her fat, meaty hands." He hung his head in shame.

"Oh, mate, "I told him, reaching out to pat him on the arm.

He raised his head and told us sadly, "And, worst of all, there were a couple of scouts there from the big clubs, looking out for new talent. And I got sent off in disgrace."

He slumped his head down onto his arms, sniffing sadly into his sleeve, as we sat back, fuming for him. The birds sang above us and the shadows lengthened on the grass as we three sat there together in silence, feeling Rob's pain, suffering with him. I was seething for my friend, but felt only deep frustration, watching distractedly as a spider climbed across Nigel's face.

The garden gate creaked open. None of us even bothered to look up to see who it was, then the visitor plonked himself roughly down beside us. Steve. He reached across the table to punch me on the arm, in his usual friendly greeting. I glanced at him, rubbing my upper arm and nodded my head back at him.

"I thought you were already inside with Jilly," I told him. He ducked his head and grinned at me.

"Just popped out to the shop," he replied, with a silly grin on his face.

I smirked back at him. "Hope it was the chemist's then," I responded. "Don't want any more little silly Jillys or sulky Steves in the world, do we?" I asked him sarcastically.

Gaz was watching Steve closely, but he twisted his face at that, and exclaimed, "Yeeww... gross. Cut it out, Will. I haven't had my tea yet."

Steve wasn't put off. Sitting back in the bench he looked casually at each one of us three, then down at Keith and Flora lying on the grass.

"So, can anyone join in this pity-party, or is it invitation only?" he asked. "What's the matter, Rob? Did Man-U not turn up today?"

Rob sniffed harder and wiped his face with his hands. I felt I should come to my mate's defence.

"Rob got sent off, Steve," I told him, expecting the air to turn blue in shock and surprise, but Steve remained calm.

"I know. I was there, watching," he told us. "I saw some of what happened before I came to find Jill. Rotten bad luck, mate, that they got to you like that."

Gaz kept staring at Steve, and frowning, like he was lip-reading him or something. I was distracted by Rob's situation and his obvious unhappiness. Rob raised his head.

"Honestly, I don't feel like I can get anything right at the moment," he told us. "Can't undo being an idiot on the pitch today, can't stand up to that witch Bernice, can't find flaming Jimmy Jesus so not making any progress there..." He tailed off, nudging Nigel with his foot.

We all seemed to slump a bit, alongside him. We were a team, in this together. I nodded my head in agreement. Gaz was the first to speak up.

"We should drop the whole idea of helping Jimmy," he stated. "Rob's searched all over town and we've not come within more than about 50 yards of him. Nobody knows where his lair is."

I looked from one of my friends to the other. Gaz was voicing the very fears we had talked about earlier. Was this our way out? Could we just paint a bridge or do a litter-pick for our Citizenship project?

Steve got to his feet, ruffling Rob's hair as he did so. "Can't find Jimmy Jesus, lads? I didn't know you were even looking for him."

I glanced up as Steve made to walk towards the house, where Jilly was waving from the kitchen window. He saw my puzzled expression and turned back to me, hands jauntily stuffed in his jeans pocket.

"H'away, lads. *Everyone* knows where to find Jimmy Jesus," he began.

We three all raised our heads to him, questioningly.

"Every Friday night, regular as clockwork, he goes to the railyard."

"What? The railyard where Mad Mick works?" I asked, unsure whether to believe him or not. This was a wind-up, surely?

"That's the one. At nine o'clock there's a fish and chip delivery, on the dot, every week," Steve said. "And every Friday night, there's an extra portion just for Jimmy. He never misses."

Steve bent down to straighten Nigel's jacket, blew him a kiss, and walked on, but he turned just before he reached the kitchen door.

"Oh, and there's always an extra sausage in there for Bernice too." He winked, chuckled, and waved up at Jilly.

And off he toddled, towards his beloved, waiting in the kitchen with a silly grin on her face.

Gaz was up on his feet by now.

"I knew something was wrong with Steve," he told us, gazing first at his retreating back, then back to us two. We raised our eyebrows at Gaz, waiting for more. We knew he'd come out with something dumb;

he usually did.

"Didn't you see?" he demanded. "Steve was wearing red lippy."

Rob actually smiled at that. Some of his earlier despair seemed to have lifted from him. He looked brighter all of a sudden, buoyed up, cheerful almost.

"That's it, lads. We're sorted now," he told us smugly.

Chapter 17

We barely slept at all that night. I worried and wondered about what was coming next. For a start, I had begun to feel some relief at getting out of the Rescuing-Jimmy-Project; we'd been so close, Gaz and me, to backing out completely, but I really didn't want to let Rob down. Or look like a Muppet in front of the rest of the Citizenship class and Mr Angus.

Later, Rob told me he had lain awake for most of the night wondering about how we could pose triumphantly with a fresh, cleanly shaved Jimmy on the front page of the Echo. He could wear his footy medals in the photo and his team shirt.

Gaz said he dreamed about choking to death on a giant marshmallow and woke up with half his pillow in his gob…

Putting together a plan for that very night wasn't as easy as we thought. It was quite momentous actually, for three lads who generally roll out of the house on a Friday with the sole intention of getting a McDonald's, trying to snog some of the girls going into the roller rink, and avoiding Big Bird and Mad Mick. But this night would be different: we were on a mission and nothing could stop us. Even the gloomy weather didn't put us off. We were close to getting our revenge *and* finding Jimmy, and the very idea made us dance with delight.

It was a bit chilly and a clammy fog had dropped by the time it began to get dark, but that just made the whole plan seem funnier in a way. We dressed Nigel in a hooded jacket, some old tracky bottoms and a pair of trainers which an aunty had bought for me but which I wouldn't be seen dead in. We didn't need to find a wig for Nigel as he was also wearing a baseball cap, backwards of course. In my bedroom we stood back from him to give him a final check over. His wrists were sticking out the end of the sleeves and glowed whitely in the gloom, his feet looked far too big for him and the tracksuit bottoms were at least two sizes too small. He looked for all the world like a proper gangly teenager. We had to laugh at him standing there propped up against my wardrobe.

"Doesn't he look like that Maths student we had in school last term?" giggled Gaz.

"He looks amazing," I said. "He looks like a real person."

"All he needs is some spots..." said Rob, picking up a felt tip.

"Oy, get off," I told him. "Our Nigel's got good skin. He knows how to take care of himself, you know. He's a model after all."

Gaz chipped in, quite seriously, "Yeah, he probably has a really healthy diet and drinks gallons of water to get skin like he's got. All the top models do. I read about it in Just Seventeen."

Rob and I smiled and shook our heads.

"Ok, lads, this is the plan," I told them. "We four go down to the railyard, make sure Gog and Magog are in there together, and frighten the life out of them."

"I thought we were going after Bernice and Mick?" Gaz said, looking perplexed.

"What? That's your plan?" asked Rob. "Quite how do we do that exactly?"

"Oh, I don't know," I retorted. "We'll work out the finer details when we get there. Let's just play it by ear. Come on, let's be off."

Together we carried Nigel down the stairs, passing my dad who was sitting at the kitchen table reading the newspaper.

"Have fun, lads," he told us without looking up. "Don't be too late."

"Oh, we will, Dad," I giggled.

You know, sometimes people can really surprise you. There we were, walking down our street thinking that someone would notice that for once there were four of us, and that the extra person looked like an alien, but no-one gave us a second glance. We all waved at old Mr Cartwright three doors down and held his gate open for him, but he just said, "Thanks. What good lads you are."

"Well, he is pretty ancient," said Rob. "Probably as blind as a bat."

We also slouched slowly past a row of women waiting at the bus stop to go to Bingo, but one of them just muttered, "Don't these kids know how stupid they look wearing their hats backwards like that?"

Another cackled loudly, "They don't need backwards 'ats to look stupid these days, Kath!"

Quite unnecessary, I thought, feeling hurt. We decided to try the corner shop. We jostled in, carrying Nigel between us, and stood in the queue.

When we got to the till I asked, "Four packets of Worcester sauce crisps please, Bal, and a packet of chewy."

Bal busily handed over the crisps, quickly scanning our faces. As he turned back with the chewing gum he said, "That'll be three pounds fifty, please, Will. Are you ok, lads?" Then to our delight his eyes widened, and he stopped with a sudden gasp. "Eeh, you gave me a right shock there. Look at the state of him. He looks dead!"

We howled in delight that finally Nigel had had the desired effect on someone. Rob lifted one of the dummy's arms and gave Bal a sort of salute whilst Gaz bent the dummy forward in a mock bow.

"Go on, get him out of here. Take him back to the graveyard before the sun comes up." The shopkeeper laughed and a few others in the queue joined in good naturedly. We left, feeling more cheerful now, knowing that if we could frighten the normally shockproof owner of the corner shop, we could certainly put the willies up Mad Mick and Big Bird.

The four of us crept close to the fence running right around the railyard and popped our heads through a few broken slats. All seemed quiet. A few empty carriages were standing in the sidings, a freight train was wrapped up tight for the night with all its tarpaulins on and there was no sign of Mick, the security guard. There was a light on in the shed the security guards used, but the windows were a little steamed up so we couldn't see who was in there. Of course, that also meant that whoever was in there couldn't quite see who was outside either.

We crouched down behind the fence, keeping a close eye out for anyone passing by who would tell us off for being so close to the railway lines. I mean, come on, we're not stupid, you know. We knew how to keep safe and all that; we just wanted to get our own back on Bernice. And Mad Mick as well, for all the months of torture he'd given us and for being dense enough to be in a relationship with Bernice. We decided to get a little closer, so we walked round to the front gates.

The railyard is out of bounds to the public, of course, and all visitors have to report to the shed near the main gate. No one is allowed near the trains or the wagons because they may tamper with them, or damage the tracks, or get run over, or electrocuted by the power lines. We knew all this; all the local kids knew this, but it was a good laugh, once in a while, to try to get past whichever sad loser was on the gate. You see, just beyond the yard there was an amazing little nature reserve with a very tempting pond for fishing in and where loads of us kids would set up temporary camps and play jungle survival games. We knew we shouldn't trespass on the railway, but if we ever did manage to get through the yard and into the reserve, the guards on the gate usually left us alone because they realized that once there, they would be left in peace. They would then go back to watching Corrers or something on their iPhones in their cosy shed.

"Ok, one of us has to get close to the window and see if Mick is actually on duty tonight," I said.

"Not me," said Rob. "He still hasn't forgiven me for putting maggots in his lunch box." He grinned at the memory.

"That was last summer!" I hissed.

"I know," Rob hissed back, "but elephants have memories like… thingumies, don't they? Gaz can go."

"I can't," wailed Gaz. "Mick plays dominoes with my dad in the club."

"So what?" I asked and all I got in response was, "Dur," like I was some kind of dummy for not having worked that out for myself.

"Nigel can go. It's his turn," Gaz said in an officious sort of voice. And the really worrying thing is, he seemed to mean it.

In the end, because the whole venture was my idea, and because it was me whom Big Bird had a death threat against, I was volunteered.

After much giggling, hissing and some false starts, I began a crouching run to the door of the shed but halfway there I turned back.

"What?" asked Rob. "You were almost there."

"I need a wee!" I hissed, laughing as though a bubble was about to burst inside me.

"No, you don't. It's just nerves," Gaz told me. "It's just like when you have to read in assembly, or when the taps are running in the bath. Go on, get out there!"

After some jiggling up and down, I decided he was right and set off again. This time I got right underneath the window. I waited for a second or two to catch my breath and to stifle any giggles which could erupt at any time. Looking back at the lads gave me confidence: Rob grinned and gave me a thumbs up; Gaz had both hands over his mouth and seemed to be laughing silently; and Nigel just lay against a tree trunk looking a bit vacant.

Quickly I popped my head up and looked into the shed. I could see Mick putting the kettle on and there she was, the evil one herself, applying lipstick with a little mirror in her hand. How she didn't turn to stone looking at her own reflection is beyond me. I beat a triumphant hasty return to the lads.

"Both of them!" I cheered.

"Yes!" they shouted quietly in unison, slapping their hands together on a joyous salute.

"Now then, lads, first things first. We'll do a quick dummy run with Nige…"

Rob started laughing.

"What?" I asked.

"Ha! Dummy run," he said, "with Nigel. Get it? Oh, never mind."

"Yeah, yeah, very funny. We'll take it in turns to run him around the shed to try to bring those two out. Rob, you first."

We positioned Rob at the main gate with Nigel, having first checked that the coast was clear. Just as they were about to set off, we all paused and dived behind the bush again. A train was slowly and smoothly, quietly edging its way into the yard from one of the sidings at the other end. It was a small freighter which soon disappeared out of sight, and I think now, when I trust myself to look back, that was the moment the blue touch paper was lit…

"Oh, bloody hell, that could spoil things. There must be people still working." I felt my heart lurch a bit.

We waited a moment longer, but there was no further sound or movement, so Rob and Nigel set off once more.

Gaz and I crouched down behind our bush, laughing quietly as we watched Rob and Nigel wobbling their way around the shed. In the misty gloom they looked really funny, like a pair of mismatched Siamese twins, with Nigel's head bobbing along as he lurched against Rob's shoulder. They got back to us and flopped down just as the shed door opened and Mick's head came out.

"Who's there?" he called in a suspicious voice. Surely, he would see the bush rocking with our silent laughter. We heard the door slam shut. None of us moved. After a second it opened again, then shut more gently this time.

"Brilliant! Your turn now, Will," Rob told me, handing Nigel over delicately. I peered out to make sure no trap had been set, then positioned Nigel comfortably and stood up. Together we darted past the window and I was dimly aware of movement from inside. Shit! Mick was on the move and I was tripping over Nige. We were going to get caught even before the fun had begun! I dropped Nigel behind some sheet metal and ran on to hide behind an abandoned wagon. Crouching down in the dark I heard the door open, more forcefully this time, and feet crunching about on the path. Then a voice rang out in the fog.

"If I find any bloody kids out here tonight, I'll make mincemeat of 'em! Bugger off home and play with your dolls, you little morons!"

He may as well have shouted, "Fee, fie, fo, fum." It set me off giggling again and wanting a pee. I slouched back to the gate when the coast was clear.

"Where's Nigel? Mick didn't get him, did he?" asked Gaz in panic.

"No, he's hiding behind the shed. He's quite safe, for now," I told him. "Phew, that was close though."

Rob took charge. "Right, we'll have to join him. We can't leave him there all by himself. Come on, quietly now."

We started to creep past the shed. I was in the middle, Rob was leading and Gaz was at the back. I glanced over my shoulder as we sneaked under the window. Gaz was on all fours: as we got to the corner of the shed, he raised his leg and pretended to pee like a dog against the wood. I sniggered, until I heard a familiar voice, like a dragon with a sore throat.

"You know what, Mick? I reckon there's still someone out there."

Bernice, with radar lugs. I bet she could hear a fly fart at 50 metres, that one. I kicked out at Gaz to speed him up and pushed Rob ahead of me. We joined Nigel behind the sheets of metal as the shed door opened once more. This time we knew they would make a more thorough search. We all glanced at each other's faces glowing palely in the dim light. Was it the cold or simple terror which made us all look so sickly?

Mick and Bernice paced about like a couple of grizzlies, snarling into the dark and making fairly obscene threats to whoever they thought may be close enough to hear them. We were just about to stand up and run for a safer spot when a third voice called out.

"Trouble, Mick?"

Aha, the train driver. We watched carefully as Bernice slid into the shadows beside the shed. Of course! She wasn't supposed to be there either! I watched as her heavy figure melted away in the mist and darkness. Ha. How many times have we wished she would do *that* permanently?

"Nah, just kids I suspect, but I've frightened them off. They won't be coming back here in a hurry. Not with the kicking they've just had off me," Mick crowed.

We looked at each other in surprise. The lying git! He and the train driver exchanged a few words then Mick went back to the shed. The train driver could be heard whistling as he went out through the main gate.

"Ok, lads, plan B. Let's get Nigel over to that train across there so we can try to lure those two out. That way, someone might spot Bernice and get them both into trouble. Mick's not supposed to be enjoying female company while he's working. Did you see her trying to hide?"

"Yes, it was like trying to conceal a hippo among a herd of sheep," laughed Rob.

Just then another train slid into the yard from way back. We hadn't even heard it coming, though it was travelling very slowly. Once inside the yard it slowed to a walking pace and gave out some metallic clunks and clanks before quietly shushing to a halt.

"Don't you think we should just pack it in and go home? We'll find Jimmy another night, eh?" asked Gaz. "There's still a few people about." He sounded worried. I felt that blue-lit fuse getting closer to it its target...

"Exactly," I told him. "We want someone to discover Bernice in Mick's shed. We'll just have to be careful, so they don't see *us*. We may even have to sacrifice Nigel, but by God it would be worth it to see those two get their comeuppance."

There was a collective sharp intake of breath at that point.

"No!" Rob and Gaz sighed in unison.

"Oh, give over you two. Can't you see the headlines? Security Guard Caught Having Sex in Shed whilst Railway Workers Watch? Or something."

"Bit long for a headline, isn't it?" Rob asked.

"*Are* they having sex while people watch, do you think?" asked Gaz, interestedly. I sighed and we put together our battle plan.

Chapter 18

Gaz knew, because he's a bit of an anorak, that one of the smaller Sprinter-type trains would be leaving the yard in a short while. It would pass within calling distance of Mick's shed. Our plan was to put Nigel on the train and make believe he was one of us, joking around where we shouldn't be. Mick would obviously come bombing out, full steam ahead, to catch us, but of course we wouldn't be on the train: we would be nearer to the shed so we could entice Bernice out as well. One of us would cause a distraction so that anyone else in the yard would also come out to see what all the fuss was about and would hopefully catch the two of them.

"Right, as Nigel is my concern, I think I should be the one to put him on the train," I stated, looking eagerly at Rob and Gaz. They nodded in agreement.

"Gaz, you can position yourself near the track so you can call out when anyone comes. Rob, you come with me and keep a look out for me while I get him onto the train."

It was all a bit vague but hey, we were a team, we had experience of being pests in this yard. We knew our way around it and weren't going to get caught. There was still a little worry ticking away at the back of my brain, if I'm honest, but I didn't feel it warranted enough attention. It would prevent us from performing our perfect plan. I tried really hard to push that negative little niggle from my head, but it just sank down a little to the back of my brain. Anyway, I decided, it was all going to be such a laugh, and worth it as well, just to see those two gorgons getting into huge trouble.

It was becoming foggier and damper as we set off into the gloom. If I'm honest, it was a bit spooky, with huge dark shapes looming at us out of the mist as we made our silent way towards the tracks. Any small crunching sounds our feet made were muffled in the fog and I felt glad that Robbo was just behind me, backing me up. I could hear him breathing quietly as I kept a tight hold of Nige.

The hair at the back of my neck stood up in anticipation of what we were about to achieve. I really didn't want to lose Nigel, but Bernice had rattled us more than once and this seemed like the perfect way to get our own back without losing too much face. Rob's footballing future could have been irreparably damaged because of that witch: we were all still livid about it – maybe me even more than Rob, on his behalf.

The Sprinter was in place, engine running but just quietly chugging away as if the driver was warming her up. He was nowhere to be seen, probably having a final fag and a cuppa before setting off. Anyway, Gaz had assured us that they rarely checked the carriages at this time of night as they expected the yard to be free of trespassers. We had sniggered at that point.

Rob, Nigel and I crouched down on the other side of the track. There was an empty line of track between us and the train. Because it was a railyard, and not a station, there were no platforms.

"Rob, make sure that track stays empty, mind. I don't fancy being made into a BillyBurger, being minced by another train as I cross over."

"No problem, mate," Rob told me. "Anyway, Gaz says this is the last train into and out of the yard tonight."

"Oh and of course Gaz is never wrong, is he?" I added, sarcastically. "Remember that time he said there was a dragon in their garage? Turned out to be a badger but he nearly convinced us two."

Rob laughed, his shoulders shaking as he tried to keep quiet. "Yeah, and what about the time he thought he bought tickets for X-Factor and ended up on Songs of Praise?"

We started one of those helpless, falling around, gasping for air sessions of laughter before we realized that the nerves were getting to us and we'd better get on with the job before this train left without Nigel. With a quick glance to left and right, I hurried the dummy across the gleaming lines of track to the train.

Placing Nigel down on the ground carefully, straightening his cap with a quick "sorry, mate", I climbed up the side and peeped into the empty carriage – I was surprised at how big these carriages were close up – and boy, was it empty! No seats, very little flooring, no overhead parcel shelves.

"Huh? What's going on here, like?"

I glanced back at Rob who gestured to me to get on with it. Leaving Nigel where he was, I tiptoed back across the track.

"What?" Rob asked. "Why didn't you do it?"

"There's something wrong with this train," I told him. "It's all empty. I don't reckon it's going anywhere. I think it's in for a refit, that's all."

"So why is the engine turning over then?" Rob asked, looking puzzled. "Look, we're running out of time. Just plonk Nigel on it and let's get out of here. Bloody Gaz must have got this all wrong."

"What, our Gaz get something wrong? Getaway," I said sarcastically before dashing back over the lines.

In my head, I should have listened to that ticking sound which was issuing me with a warning… This place was seriously spooky at this time of night. There were strange sounds, hisses, steam floating about in the air like spectral apparitions. I gave my head a shake and continued on my mission.

Nigel seemed pale and felt cold and clammy when I touched him.

"Ok, fella, up you go."

I managed to get his head and shoulders in through the open window then I noticed that the bottom part of one of his legs had come unscrewed again and was almost hanging off.

"Oh, what the..." I began, when I heard a noise from both Rob and the other side of the train. Looking over my shoulder Rob was just visible where he was crouching. He was making steering wheel gestures and pointing to the front end of the train. Oh no, the driver was getting on and Nigel was only just hanging out of the window! With a slam the door into the driver's compartment shut, the brakes were eased off and the train began to move slowly forward.

I nearly died, I can tell you! It's not funny being that close to a moving train, in the fog, in the dark, standing in the middle of a railway track. Without looking behind, I jumped back and fell, catching my footing on the lines. I lay there like an idiot thinking, shit – is one of these rails electrified? I could fry here, and no-one could do anything to help me. I rubbed at my twisted foot and tried to stand up, watching as the sprinter slowly chugged away with Nigel still hanging out of the window. His broken lower leg was swinging, and despite everything I laughed at the sight of him. He looked just like someone trying to break in!

Suddenly, from somewhere behind me, I heard a familiar bellow. Mick was on the move! And he wasn't alone. Another man's voice could be heard from opposite where I was, yelling blue murder – the sort of words your mam would kill you for even knowing, let alone using.

I backed off the track and tried to hide beside Rob.

We flew a couple of metres to a spot behind some old wheels and watched breathlessly.

"Phew, I thought you were a gonna there, mate!" Rob told me. "But Nigel looks amazing. Gaz has done his bit. Mick's on his way and there's enough men out now to catch Bernice."

"Yeah, but hopefully not us!" I laughed, watching the approach of Mick the security guard. He was running towards the train, waving his fists and shouting, but the sprinter driver obviously couldn't hear him. Poor bugger, I thought, getting all het up and foaming at the mouth 'cos he thinks someone is getting onto one of his precious trains. Oh, this was good.

Rob and I rocked in silent mirth as we watched Mick stumble along the lines. He actually moved quite quickly for a big bloke as well, because in next to no time he had caught the train up and had made a grab for Nigel's swinging foot.

"You bloody idiot! What the hell do you think you're playing at? Are you trying to get killed?" he yelled, trying to yank Nigel out of the window. Rob and I stood up to get a better view.

"Oh, this just gets better." I nudged Rob. "Look!"

Bernice was waddling towards the track too now, shouting something to her beloved.

"Gotcha!" I said in quiet triumph. "Look, Rob." I nudged my mate, but he wasn't there.

Rob was heading forward, at a low crouch, aiming for the train. "Rob, man," I hissed. "Get back here. What are you doing?"

Rob slowed slightly, just enough to whisper back over his shoulder. "I'm getting Nigel. I'm not leaving him for those two to tear apart. Keep a look out for the other guards arriving to nick Big Bird." Then he grinned, gave me a thumbs up, and ran on, giggling, ever the hero.

At that very moment, another sprinter slipped onto the track on our side, heading straight for Mick and Nigel. Boom.

Mick was so busy trying to pull our dummy out of the window that he didn't see or hear the train until it was almost on top of him. Rob reached Mick, looming out of the mist just as the driver of the new train spotted what was going on at the last minute and frantically screeched the brakes on, but it was too late. I tried to shout. I tried to look away. I was frozen to the spot. I saw it all. Mick flung his hands up to his face as if to protect himself, and he screamed in fear, sounding like a wounded lion. He reached out to make a grab for Rob who seemed as if he was moving in slow motion, such was the effect of the lights from the train and the swirling mist.

Suddenly Rob turned to look over his shoulder. His face froze, he lurched to one side. His eyes and face scrunched up. He tumbled over, down into the cold darkness onto the track. I watched in horror as he sort of gradually crumpled in on himself. As he was dragged under the wheels of the train. The last thing I saw was his terrified face. Wild eyes. Open mouth. The noise he made, and the sound of the train's brakes screaming, will never be erased from my mind. That image was burned onto my eyes and branded onto my brain. I will see it forever. I will never shake it off.

All at once people were running, shouting, screaming, for help, for an ambulance. Lights seemed to be going on and everything happened as if it was in a film. The mist swirled around and added to the unreal effect. I stood frozen. I wanted to run away but shock and horror held me captive. Gaz appeared at my side, whimpering like a puppy in pain. I think he was sick. He suddenly flopped down to the ground at my feet and put his head in his hands. I tried to speak but my mouth was locked in a grimace. Then a female voice could be heard screaming like a trapped animal.

"No, no, no, no! Mick! No!"

Bernice. Someone was holding her back and leading her away from the horror that was underneath that train.

After a minute or two, which felt like eternity, I found myself stumbling towards the light like a zombie. My brain was certainly as dead as a zombie's, as dead as Mick's surely must be. Where was Rob? Where was my hero best mate? I was so terrified I couldn't breathe normally and my legs wouldn't carry me forward to find him.

I got fairly close to the nightmare scene before someone realized I was there.

"No, kid. Get away from here! What do you think you're playing at?"

A man wearing the Railway workers' donkey jacket put an arm around me and pulled me roughly away, turning my head towards his shoulder. Too late. I had already seen it. The blood, the severed limbs, the mush on the track and splashed up against the train doors. The smell! Oh God – that smell. Of death?

"I was only playing. I didn't know. I didn't think…." I sobbed, allowing them to carry me like a dummy to a waiting police officer.

Chapter 19

M e, Rob and Gaz were never quite the same again after that. Our lives were damaged beyond repair and the once jokey camaraderie didn't ever come so easily to us again. We were suddenly older, outsiders, criminals. No one wanted to speak to us: I could understand. They didn't know what to say. *I* didn't know what to say. The shockwaves of that incident will rumble through our lives forever. I don't think the pain will ever recede.

Our families were certainly in deep shock, our teachers were speechless, but some tried to encourage us to continue studying for our GCSEs. That was a waste of time: we failed the lot, worrying about the court case we all had to face, all that publicity. Again.

I couldn't begin to tell you about how all this affected Bernice. Her parents moved her away to another town. I can't even think about her face and her rigid reaction to the accident without throwing up and starting the sleepless nights off again.

Mick was badly damaged. He lost a lot of blood and spent weeks in hospital. Gaz went to visit him in there. I was amazed by that. Of all of us, Gaz – he really grew up and was prepared to take whatever consequences were coming our way. He asked me to go with him, of course, to the hospital to see Mick, but I was still in hiding, staying away from a world that had come crashing down around me. I couldn't face anyone.

I felt totally responsible for what happened to Mick. I had been so blinded by my pointless revenge, and really, when all is said and done, the guy was just doing his job. He was making a living, trying to keep stupid kids like us out of danger. And the accident had a lasting effect on him too. He was offered a transfer when he recovered to another job on the trains, but last I heard he had moved to Scotland and was working as a pig farmer. In another, happier time, I would have made a huge joke of that... Poor Mick. I'm so sorry, mate, for everything I put you through.

Rob. My hero, my best mate, the sporting superstar with a lively career ahead of him. He lost the lower part of his right leg and seriously damaged a hand. His face was scarred but they should fade in time. It's ironic to think that my friend ended up losing part of his leg, like Nigel did, and damaged his face too, like Keith. His memories won't fade though, because he lost a lot more. He lost all his body confidence, his swagger, his jokey sense of fun, his close friendship with me. Well, he was like a brother to me, especially after I had already lost Ross, my older brother, only a couple of years earlier.

Rob spent weeks in hospital and then had to have further surgery and months of physio, learning how to walk. We wanted him to have one of those sports blades fitted to his limb, because that would really suit the sort of person Rob was. He would be the cool kid again, dashing and different. But Rob wasn't going to be dashing anywhere anymore, and the crutches and stumpy rubber foot were ugly and hard to manage.

Oh yes, girls still wanted to talk to him, but now there was sadness and pity in their eyes, not pride and interest in him as a person in his own right. He was a marked man, crippled, not only physically, but emotionally too. He'd sort of shrunk, become a smaller version of himself. And the sad thing is that, although I visited him regularly in hospital, that awful injury freaked me out. Rob was doing better with it than I was. Even the word was horrendous: stump. I couldn't look at it; couldn't say it. Rob must have thought I was going totally woke, holding his hand and gazing into his eyes when I was by his bed. In truth, I was avoiding looking at how damaged my mate was. And all because of a laugh, a bit of fun, in completely the wrong place.

And then, to add insult to injury, after three weeks in hospital he got a letter offering him a place at the Football Academy for Sunderland AFC. That was a real kick in the teeth. We all cried for him. Again. I tried my best to cheer him up and be a friend to him, but the Rob I knew and loved wasn't really there any longer. Neither was I, to be honest.

All my bottled memories of losing our Ross came flooding back to haunt me, as if I needed a reminder of that painful time. I was worried about the effect of this accident on my mam and dad. Jilly came good for me, surprisingly. My parents had been through enough already, and although I wasn't physically hurt, unlike Mick and Rob, I simply sank again. I think for a few weeks I was like a nine-year-old, wandering around, crying, forgetting to eat. It's like that song – it only hurts when I breathe.

This time, my mam was the strong one. She still had me, you see. That was all that mattered to her. I was still here, her baby, in one piece, at least physically, if not emotionally and mentally. Instead of being distant and vague, as she had been when Ross died, with me she became clingy. She couldn't stop grabbing me for a cuddle, squeezing me till I almost turned blue. I just about stopped her from holding my hand to cross the road again.

It was my dad who fell apart this time. He went to work every day, for a while, but he simply couldn't focus. He became a danger on the Production Line, and was often away from his station, meaning cars were going on to the next position with bits missing, whilst my dad gazed out of the windows with tears on his face. He felt he was no longer in charge of the tools he used, the instructions he had to follow, and after a few weeks he "took some time off, on the sick". He found solace in the pub for a while, but between Jilly and my mam we got him back again before too much damage was done. He took up gardening once more, and our once rough but colourful patch became cool, soft, pretty and well-tended. I noticed Dad was often in the shed – "attending to his tools" he said – but I often caught the flicker of candlelight in there in the evenings. He had taken to chatting to Ross, where in the past he thought I was odd for doing exactly that.

Father O'Rafferty was great, again. That guy is nearly a saint, I tell you. He came to help the family in any way he could, not preaching or even praying, just little practical acts of kindness and generosity. Obviously having him around was too much for my mam, at first. It took her back to losing Ross again, but Raff's gentle manner and soothing presence got the better of her and she turned to him as an interested and experienced outsider. He became the glue which stuck us all back together again.

Ross had been our family superstar. The first member of the Green family to go to Uni, clever and handsome, funny and stylish. He was studying for a degree in Fine Art and Design. He wasn't quite brave enough to go off to another city to study so he stayed local. He used to say, *why should I leave? Everything I love and need is here, my family, our beautiful beach, my mates.*

He loved Uni, loved his lectures, the relaxed lifestyle... but someone in his new circle of friends persuaded him to try drugs on a night out. Ross didn't even smoke; he didn't do drugs; he wasn't like that. He collapsed in the street and was rushed to hospital foaming at the mouth, swollen and bloated like a dead fish. MDMA. It killed him.

He died in the same hospital that we took Jimmy to. The staff were fantastic, tried everything in their power to bring Ross back to who he really was, but it was no good. I think the nursing staff and the medical team were as devastated as we were. Nobody was ever charged over his death; there wasn't enough evidence that Ross had been spiked they said. It was just bad luck on his behalf. An accident. A warning to others.

Ah, Jimmy. Once again, Fr O'Rafferty to the rescue. He took charge of Jimmy, who had earlier escaped from his hospital ward. Raff and his team searched the city for him and found him. He had a little lair, right underneath Monkwearmouth Bridge, which is where Rob and Gaz had spotted him going to that night on the bus.

In one of our "chats" with Raff, Gaz and I mentioned that we had plans to improve Jimmy's life through our school project. He laughed loudly, roaring in a good-natured fashion, before asking the sort of questions we should have asked ourselves. I was mortified.

"We were stupid, Raff." I told him, head bowed so he couldn't see my embarrassment. Raff sat back in his chair in our kitchen and placed his cup of tea very gently on the table.

"Stupid, Will? Why would you say that?" he asked gently, his eyes raking over my face.

I puffed out my cheeks, rubbing my face with my hands. I felt so ashamed. In my head I was thinking about how on board I had really been with the whole Jimmy Rescue. It had seemed brilliant at the time, something really worthwhile to get our teeth into, and an attempt to help the old guy at the same time, but we were sadly lacking in the planning stages and that always worried me. It had freaked me out, if I'm honest. There were gaps in the crucial development stage that we weren't equipped to deal with. We three had just blundered our way through it.

"Father Raff," I began, searching for how to explain my mixed emotions. "We were out of our depth, weren't we? And we were too stupid and pig-headed to ask for help. We thought we could rescue Jimmy, help make his life better, but we just seemed to add to his troubles."

I took a long slurp of my own mug of tea, trying to avert my eyes from the big priest's kind face. He wasn't fooled for a moment. Reaching across the table he patted my hand.

"Will, it *was* a brilliant idea. And you know, you're being too hard on yourselves. You were only teenagers, but you had Jimmy's wellbeing and safety at heart. I loved it when I eventually heard what you three tried to do for that old chap."

I looked up at him then. He was grinning at me, openly, genuinely.

"How many other people do you know of, Will, who have ever put Jimmy before themselves?" he asked, eyebrows raised. "Jimmy is just a figure of fun to most people," he continued. "They avoid him. They shun him. They actually set out to hurt him in some cases."

His voice became serious. I studied his dark handsome face.

"You treated Jimmy with kindness, respect and even love, Will. You three worried about him and got him some help. How many kids of your age even bothered with Jimmy? You are heroes in my eyes, Will. Don't ever put yourself down for trying to do good."

I smiled at him and shrugged my shoulders. Yeah, maybe he was right. Raff recognized our panic about the old chap. He could see that, good intentioned as we were, it was all just too much for us to handle without expert help. And Fr O'Rafferty became our expert.

The relief I felt was HUGE. I was finally able to breathe; I was like a drowning man coming up for air. Once Raff stepped in, I was able to focus on Rob, Gaz, my family. Oh, and eventually myself. Raff arranged for Jimmy to attend Peter's Place regularly, for food, clothing and company. Gaz still sees Jimmy there and Jimmy looks quite different. He still doesn't really communicate properly with the other guests, but he's clean and safe. Rumour has it there's a bed coming up for him in the Care Home the Sisters of Mercy run. Raff again, doing his thing, bless him.

So, that just leaves me, Will. I suppose I'll also get there, in the end, but it seems a long way off. I did spend some time wondering about where "there" really was: is it a safe place for my troubled mind to visit once in a while? For Rob, is it a place of physical comfort, where he can forget about what happened, and can also forget about the plans he once had?

A few weeks after the accident I came out in hives, I suppose they'd call it. Huge itchy lumps came up, all over my body and my limbs. I couldn't go out of the house for ages, which was ok, because I still couldn't face the world. Steve didn't help by referring to me as the Elephant Man, but Jilly soon put him back in his place with a swift back-hander.

I can now, just occasionally, look back and smile at some of the daft tricks we lads got up to. It's weird, you know. Sometimes it's like it happened last week, when in reality it's nearly a year now. I can't get my head around it. Some mornings I wake up and forget it really happened, then I bounce out of bed to start the day with a smile. It soon fades though, that smile. Other days, even months later, I can't get out of bed in the first place...

The dummies, Keith, Nigel and Flora very quietly faded away after that disastrous night. I know the police hung onto Nigel as evidence, for a while, before he was quietly 'disposed of' without fuss or ceremony. Keith was returned to the bins in Dooley's by our Jilly and probably resides in a landfill site somewhere, being raked over by rats and seagulls. Flora was donated to a local Drama group, and last I heard she was starring in the lead role in Annie, the Musical, or something.

Fr O'Rafferty's charity Fashion Show went ahead without us. It was a lively affair apparently, and some of the lovely local girls donated some money towards a new false limb for Rob. Fiona Bridges even visited him in the hospital one night, taking him a card and grapes, sitting on his bed and ruffling his hair. She cheered him up much more than Gaz or I ever could. Honestly, that lad. If he fell into a sewer, I swear he would be washed out to sea and land on a sunlit beach somewhere surrounded by singing, semi-naked mermaids.

As we left the hospital that night, leaving Rob in the capable hands of Fiona, Gaz and I paused at the ward door and looked back at the two of them. Rob was showing Fiona something on his mobile. Their heads were very close together and they were smiling and pointing at an image on the screen. For a moment, the background disappeared – the beds, the uniforms, the machines and medicines – and the two of them seemed happily frozen in their own little tableau. I gulped, my eyes smarting with tears.

"He'll be fine, you know, Will." Gaz placed a warm hand on my shoulder. "Our Rob will come though this fine. And so will we. We have to be strong."

I tried to smile hopefully back at my mate as we left the building.

I miss the dummies. But that is a part of my life I have locked away in a very dark vault. There is a key, somewhere, but, at the moment, it's simply too scary to find it and open up that particular Pandora's box. I take a load of tablets, go to counselling, have some therapy, try to study for my re-sits.

When I'm having a really dark day, I scroll through the photos on my iPhone, looking at the crazy stuff us lads got up to with Keith, Nigel and Flora. There's a great one I sneaked of Jilly, putting on her make-up in the bathroom mirror. Her face is an absolute picture because she had just spotted Nige sitting on the toilet behind her, trousers round his ankles. That can still make me smile. And the one my mam took in secret, of Keith sitting on the garden bench, seeming to hold a rake whilst my dad was bent down next to him, doing some weeding. The lads have their own photos they go to, to remind us of happier days.

The drugs don't work – honest. They are just terrifying – mine, and the ones Ross mistakenly took. When I hear of stupid kids playing and messing about on railway lines, I go all cold and clammy. I want to grab them by the throat and MAKE them look inside my head. If they could do that, they'd never go near the place again. The people who work there, who take responsibility for our travel and safety, deserve a medal. Those are huge, scary machines. What these people do *not* deserve is stupid, thoughtless kids breaking the law, putting everyone at risk and damaging lives and property. We have a huge court case coming up; we ruined our lives and our futures because this thing will never leave us. We are marked for life. And for what? For a laugh, for our own immature entertainment.

If I could go back to that fateful night, look at us three with Nigel from the safety of the bridge outside of the railyard, I would tell myself, Rob and Gaz only one thing: you only get one chance at life, you know. Use your head. Don't be a dummy.

The End

Acknowledgements

There are a few people I would like to thank on this long and, at times, frustrating journey.

I actually wrote the first draft Dummy Run in about 2004, when I was still teaching full time and fully immersed in the crazy lives of teenagers. However, my PC was accidentally wiped, and then I lost the memory stick it was saved on. Nightmare!

Years later, I found the memory stick in the boot of my car, underneath the spare wheel. It was a surprising delight to read the story again and I set about developing it and adding to the original story. However, I was no longer teaching by then, and I worried that I would struggle to accurately pick up the narrative voice again. I was massively assisted in this by the wonderful Gina Blaxil, from Cornerstones, who acted as my editor, guide and mentor. She pointed out minor errors and offered much-needed encouragement. I couldn't have done it without her. I was also assisted by sensible observations from Network Rail, particularly Dawn Sweeting who does amazing work in schools, cautioning pupils about trespassing on the railways, and Richie Liddell, then of British Transport Police, who offered practical advice and some historical detail to be aware of.

Many thanks also to the team at UK Book Publishing, to Ruth, Jay and Dan, for all your support, and most especially the amazing cover.

The Pandemic and surgery slowed down the whole process, but finally – here we are. I hope you enjoy it. Do let me know via my Facebook page; all comments and encouragements gratefully accepted!

Annie Flanagan

www.ingramcontent.com/pod-product-compliance
Lightning Source LLC
Chambersburg PA
CBHW032008170626

46807CB00006B/2709